The Peanut Butter Twist

Tails of Maple Ridge
Book 1

Ellie Webster

Tails of Maple Ridge Series

The Peanut Butter Twist

Paws and Prejudice

The Peanut Butter Twist

ELLIE WEBSTER

Recipe for Peanut Butter Twists

Ingredients *(12–16 twists)*

Filling

- ½ cup (120 g) smooth or crunchy peanut butter
- ¼–⅓ cup (85–110 g) honey
- ¼ cup (55 g) brown sugar (optional, for extra sweetness)
- 1 tsp ground cinnamon
- 2 tbsp unsalted butter, softened or melted

Dough & Coating

- 1 sheet ready-rolled puff pastry (about 10 × 10 in / 25 × 25 cm)
- 1–2 tbsp milk, or beaten egg (for brushing)
- Granulated sugar (for sprinkling)

Instructions
1. Prep & Fill

Preheat the oven to 200°C (180°C fan). In a small bowl, whisk together peanut butter, honey, brown sugar (if using), cinnamon, and butter until smooth and spreadable.

2. Roll & Spread

Unfurl the puff pastry sheet on a lightly floured surface. Smooth the peanut butter–honey mixture over the pastry, leaving a small margin around the edges to prevent overflow when twisting.

3. Fold & Slice

Fold one short side of the pastry over to just meet the other short side, creating a double-layer strip. Press gently to seal the seam. Then cut vertically into 12–16 even strips.

4. Twist & Prepare for Baking

Twist each strip several times (2–3 twists should do) and place on a non-stick baking tray or one lined with baking paper. Press down the ends to prevent unravelling. Brush lightly with milk, or egg wash, then sprinkle with a little granulated sugar for sparkle and crunch.

5. Bake

Bake in the preheated oven for 18–20 minutes, or until puffed and golden. Watch carefully toward the end to avoid over-browning.

6. Finish & Serve

Remove from the oven and let cool for a few minutes. If desired, dust with icing sugar or drizzle with peanut butter icing. Serve warm or at room temperature.

Chapter 1

A New Page

The scent of freshly brewed espresso mingled with peanut butter twists and old books, a combination I now associated with comfort, chaos, and the occasional existential crisis. It had been six months since I'd bought the Book Mark, a dusty old bookstore in Maple Ridge, a cute college town in northern New Hampshire.

It wasn't like I'd set out to buy the place; I'd just kind of fallen in love with it. I'd needed a change after the disaster that was Boston, so I'd come out this way for a break, to recharge my batteries and figure out what I really wanted out of life. I'd actually been on my way to a resort on a lake ten miles over when I'd stumbled upon Maple Ridge.

I can't explain it, but something about the town spoke to me. Maybe it was the quaint New England architecture, or the incredible breakfasts at Mo's Diner, or how friendly everybody was.

There was also an air of academia around the place that I loved and was familiar with, since my father used to be an English Lit professor. It reminded me of home.

Then I saw it.

A faded "For Sale" sign in the window of a bookstore tucked between a bakery and a hair salon. The shutters were closed, the trim was chipped, and the blue paint had faded to a shy grey.

But there was something about it. The kind of place that felt forgotten but not unloved—like it was waiting for someone.

So I bought it.

The Book Mark, as it turned out, needed far more work than I'd bargained for. But I've always had a soft spot for lost causes—especially the literary kind—so I rolled up my sleeves and brought it back to life. I even added a little coffee bar and a cozy reading nook to make it feel more inviting... and to tempt more people through the door.

And now, here we were. Opening night.

I adjusted a crooked display of signed paperbacks while Luke, a criminology student and my only staff member, laid out a tray of cupcakes supplied by Henry next door.

"Think she'll be a diva?" he asked, dabbing a swirl of maple buttercream on the last cupcake.

I glanced toward the small podium set up at the front of the café, where a stack of the evening's featured novel sat beside a vintage lamp. "She's a historical romance writer from Vermont, Luke, not a Kardashian. Let's keep the cynicism mild—we've got polite academia in the house."

Luke snorted but offered a crooked smile. The place was already filling with my guests—an assortment of Maple Ridge locals and small business owners who I thought it might be a good idea to get to know better. After all, I was part of the community now.

Gina, the town optician, was the first to arrive. Casually dressed in jeans and a pale pink sweater that clashed with her red hair, she hurried over to where I was standing and surprised me with a hug. "I love what you've done with the place," she gushed. "I always hoped someone would buy it and transform it. We were really worried it would get sold to a developer and turned into condos or something dreadful."

"We" being the townsfolk, I guessed.

"How awful," I shuddered as I hugged her back.

"This—" she released me and waved a hand in the air— "this is amazing."

"Thank you. Would you like a coffee while we wait for our guest author? Luke here can make you whatever you want."

Luke gave a crooked grin and nodded to the fancy barista machine that had cost me a small fortune. My attention was diverted as Professor Riley arrived, still wearing his academic robes. He was an esteemed biologist at the university and liked everyone to know it. He'd been in here a few times asking me if I'd stock copies of his latest book, *Through the Canopy*, when it was released. Apparently, it contained groundbreaking research that was expected to wow the botanical world.

"Your wife not joining you tonight, Professor?" I asked as he came to a stop at the display table. His forehead creased as if he was disappointed not to find his own book on it.

"Er, no. Jessica has one of her migraines. She sends her apologies."

I'd met her too, a tiny, birdlike woman with an interest in ornithology, when they'd come in last time.

"Oh, I hope she's feeling better soon."

He grunted and helped himself to a cupcake.

Next came Sophie Beaumont from Sweet Sophisticates, the patisserie just down the block. She wore a tailored coat that screamed Parisian chic and carried a tray of macarons that screamed edible bribes. "I thought I'd contribute something more refined than cupcakes," she said with a pointed smile.

I took them gratefully. "Our cupcakes will try not to feel inferior." Henry's cupcakes, to be accurate, but luckily Henry wasn't here yet.

Peter Lane, the charming restaurateur and owner of Flint + Flame, entered with flair and a bottle of local sparkling cider. Peter was about forty, slender but with broad shoulders, classic good looks, and he stood out in the crowd—especially in those slacks and that expensive sports jacket.

Peter's place was pretty famous, or so I was told. In the evenings, Flint + Flame had a waiting list, which meant I hadn't tried it myself. I was pleased he'd deemed my little bookstore worthy of his presence, since he didn't look the type to be into historical fiction.

Lindy Huang followed close behind him. A research scientist by trade, Lindy had swapped her lab coat for an oversized pink cardigan and well-worn jeans for the evening. You wouldn't guess it by looking at her, but according to Luke, she'd practically rewritten the book on forensic science, especially when it came to blood analysis.

"I came for the cupcakes," she declared, nodding at the counter. "And the murder talk, obviously."

"You do realize this is historical fiction?" I replied with a grin. Lindy had been one of the first to welcome me to town, other than Henry, and we'd met for coffee several times since then. We shared an obsession with mystery novels.

Henry Dawson bustled in a few minutes later, red-faced and cheerful. He still had a smudge of flour on his forehead and smelled like cinnamon. "Sorry I'm late, Tess. I had to run home and change. Hope you don't mind, I brought Cocoa."

I smiled and gave the black Lab a pat on the head. Since the first day I'd met Henry, the dog had been by his side. The two were inseparable. "So glad you could make it. And thank you for the cupcakes—they're going down a treat." The tray on the counter was already half empty.

He beamed. "Least I could do, seeing as you restored this wonderful old place. And, well... you're my favorite customer."

I felt my cheeks grow warm. "Thanks, Henry." I ordered pastries from his bakery every morning, and either he or his assistant Suzanne would drop them off just before opening.

"Who brought those?" Uh-oh. He'd spotted the macarons.

"Sophie," I said, bracing for the response.

"That woman," he muttered, the smile disappearing in a flash, "never misses an opportunity to outdo me." Then he went to sit down on a vacant chair at the back. I swear the dog shot me an accusatory look before making itself comfortable by Henry's side.

Several more people had arrived, and the bookstore was almost full. "I think everyone's here," I said to Luke, trying to suppress the sudden butterflies in my stomach. I probably shouldn't have had that last cappuccino. "Let's begin."

I gave the author, Dolores Hartman, a warm welcome and thanked everyone for coming. The crowd responded with polite applause and some audible chewing.

As Dolores launched into a passage about forbidden love during the War of 1812, I scanned the crowd from my post near the espresso machine, and my heart swelled. I'd done it. I'd actually taken the sad, old bookstore and converted it into something I was proud of. Something my father would have been proud of too.

Luke leaned over the counter and whispered, "Not bad for a Friday night in a town with one traffic light."

I grinned. He was right—this was a great turnout. I realized I was happy. Happier than I'd been in a long time.

"Where's your buddy?" I whispered back. This morning

Luke had asked if his friend could come, probably for the free cupcakes.

"I don't know. Guess he changed his mind."

I nodded distractedly. The dog was lying with its head on Henry's foot, eyes on Dolores, and I would bet good money it was listening to what she was saying.

After an interesting twenty minutes, Dolores finished up, and I returned to the front and thanked her for being our first ever guest speaker. A few people bought her latest book and lined up to get it signed, while others went to the bar to order a hot drink and devour another cupcake before departing.

I stood near the door to thank everyone for coming. A middle-aged couple approached. The woman, who had hair shot through with silver, was wearing a brilliant magenta scarf and had a warm, friendly smile. Her husband, a broad, stocky man with graying hair and laugh lines, stood a few feet behind her.

"Oh, hello." She thrust out a hand. "I'm Carly, and this is my husband, Bert. We just wanted to introduce ourselves and say how glad we are you've bought this old place."

I shook her hand, breaking into a smile. "Thank you. It's great to meet you too. I'm Tess."

"We heard it was going to be torn down and turned into condos," Bert said, stepping forward.

"But we're so glad it was you who bought it instead," Carly added hurriedly. "We both work at the college. I'm an art lecturer, and Bert is a classics professor."

"Ah, classics," I said wistfully. "My father was an English professor, but he loved the classics. He used to tell me stories about ancient heroes and monsters when I was little. My favorite was Theseus and the Minotaur. He always told me that one when I couldn't sleep."

"Smart man," beamed Bert.

"How did the condo rumor start?" I asked. There'd been no hint of that when I'd put in my offer. The lawyer had said the owners were desperate to sell.

"Oh, I think that was Peter Lane's idea. He... collects run-down buildings and renovates them before renting them out or selling them on. He was interested in the bakery too, but Henry turned him down, of course."

"The restaurateur?" I was surprised; he'd seemed so charming.

"Don't let his smooth charisma fool you," Bert warned. "Beneath that expensive smile beats a Byzantine heart."

"Thanks for the advice."

"I am not trying to steal your customers." Sophie's voice rose above the crowd. I glanced around as Henry's dog emitted a low growl. A few more customers thanked me and left. I smiled at them before heading over to where Henry was facing off with Sophie.

"What do you call this?" Henry swept a hand toward the macarons.

"A gift," she smirked, then turned her back on him. "Thank you, Tess. I think it's time I left."

"I'll walk you out," Luke said, leading her to the door, while I stood between Henry, his dog, and the French woman.

"You okay?" I asked Henry.

The baker shook his head. "She's been doing that for over a decade," he said, glaring after her. "Every time I get a new customer, she tries to steal them out from under me. I'm sick of it."

I put a reassuring hand on his arm. "I'd never betray you, Henry. You know that. You were my first friend in Maple Ridge. I'm eternally grateful. Besides, nobody makes peanut butter twists like you do."

His dog licked his chops in response.

Dolores was packing up. I excused myself and went over to her as the other guests left. As I helped her to her car with the leftover books, I couldn't help thinking how even small towns had their drama.

If only I'd known then how right I was.

Chapter 2

A Troubling Twist

Cocoa

Come on, Henry!

He was always so slow. I was at the door, ready to go, and he was still putting his shoes on. I had been holding my bladder all night. Anxious didn't even begin to cover it.

When he finally opened the door, I made a beeline to my favorite lamppost. It was *my* lamppost. I knew that it belonged to me because I marked it every morning.

Just as I was about to reclaim it, I smelled something I wasn't expecting. Someone else had marked this. I thought it was the boxer down the street. I hadn't met him yet, but he barked a lot—not that he had anything worthwhile to say.

He couldn't have this post; it was mine. I marked it again after a full night in my human's bedroom. Plenty to reclaim it with, and enough left for the next post. No boxer was going to muscle in on my turf.

Between lampposts, I kept my nose glued to the ground. I was hoping for a scent of Iris. I had gotten to see her yesterday, when Henry went to pick up those funny things he wore over his eyes when he was reading. I had gotten a glimpse of that long, fluffy tail, and it had about made my day.

Henry had finally locked the door and was walking toward me, leash in hand, although he rarely needed it. I never strayed far.

About time! Don't get me wrong, I loved Henry. He was my first human, the only human I had ever known. He had taken me in when I was a pup, and I had been with him ever since.

He gave the best ear scratches, and even head pats were special—though he kept asking me, "Who's a good boy?" What was I supposed to say to that? It was the same answer every time. Me, of course. You'd think he would have known that by now.

"Come on, Cocoa," he said and waved me off in the right direction. Not that I needed it. I already knew the way. We did this every day.

The sun was breaking on the horizon, and the light shone off the closed stores and houses that lined the sleepy streets. Sometimes it felt like me and my human were the only ones awake. The world still snoozed all around us, and it was nice because it was just us.

Henry was my best friend, after all.

Sometimes we ran into the neighbor's cat. That always made for a fun morning, though Henry would get a bit shouty when I launched myself after the feral miscreant. I didn't know what he got so fussed about. I always came back. He didn't seem to get that running a cat down was a great way to get the blood pumping and start a new day. Besides, the cat asked for it—honest. He was always talking nonsense about me. Worse, he'd said some nasty things about Henry too. I wouldn't stand for that.

Anyway, it wasn't the cat that morning that interrupted our walk. I was right next to Henry, being helpful like I always was. I was keeping a close eye out for stray squirrels or rabbits or other clear threats to my human when I spotted another human across the lake.

It wasn't that unusual. Every so often we met someone before the sun came up, but they were normally running or sitting with a pole dangling in the water. Sometimes I got a head scratch and a kind word. Other times they wanted to know "Who's a good boy?" too, which was odd because, after all, I was. Still, I let them pet me. It was a public service I provided.

This one didn't come near us though. He was just standing there, staring into the water. I felt Henry bristle. He stopped, stared across the lake, then gasped. I didn't like that sound. Henry was upset.

I growled softly. My tail dropped and I locked my legs. That human over there mustn't come anywhere near Henry. My hackles rose and my lips crawled up my teeth. I couldn't help it. It was a natural reaction and not one I could control.

"Easy, boy," Henry said, patting me on the head. I relaxed a little, but I still didn't like it. I glanced up at him. *Let's go, Henry.* Something about this smelled off.

The whole situation felt weird. We were too far away for me to get a read on the person, although a familiar scent was wafting across on the morning air. It was disturbing. Smelled of something sharp—aggression, maybe? Hate? Anger? I wasn't sure; it was difficult to catalog scents, but whatever was coming off him, it was wrong.

I hung back behind Henry's knees, at the ready. I didn't actually know what it was I was ready for, but I was ready anyway.

"Come on, Cocoa," Henry said, and we hurried along the path. The stranger didn't acknowledge us, although I knew he could see us. He kept sneaking glimpses our way, but he didn't approach. I smelled fear on him. Good. I was proud that he knew I was ready to defend my human.

Henry turned back toward town, and I was happy to be leaving the stranger behind. But Henry wasn't paying attention. I stayed really close to him to make sure he didn't walk off the path or wander off somewhere. After all, I hadn't had breakfast yet, and I would have hated to have to go and find him on an empty stomach.

I tried to make him smile. I looked up at him while we were walking, but he didn't look down at me. He just kept his eyes straight ahead and gritted his teeth so hard I could hear them cracking. I really couldn't tell if he smelled angry or scared, but either way, I didn't like it. Whatever was going on with him, it was bad. Real bad. I dropped my tongue out of the side of my mouth and looked up at him with my head tilted. That look always made him smile, and he smelled so much better when he was smiling. It was my goofiest look. But that day it only got a glimmer of his normally sunny grin.

Stay close.

The thought was so intense, I pressed in tightly. I walked in silence, but close enough that sometimes my side rubbed against his leg. That at least let him know I was there without being too disruptive. Sometimes Henry just liked to be alone with his thoughts, and all I could do was pad alongside him. I didn't really mind that. At least I got to be with him.

He opened the bakery door and switched on the lights. I ran inside, just like I always did. I was allowed in the front section with all the glass and the displays of baked goodness, but not in the back. That was where the best smells came from, but Henry didn't want me in there. I knew better than to push. While things smelled good in there, eventually they got moved to the front where I could get at them.

I hoped he made peanut butter twists this morning. That was my favorite. Both the smell and the taste were wonderful. I would have begged for a good peanut butter twist any day of the week. Just sweet enough, but not too sweet—perfection in soft dough filled with peanut buttery goodness.

Fine, I would have begged for anything in those wonderful cases. But the peanut butter twists? There was just something about them.

Henry didn't disappoint. When he brought me my breakfast and set my bowl behind the counter, I could see he had put a little crumble of peanut butter twist on top of the kibble. He gave me a good scratch behind the ears, just where I liked it, and then patted my head.

Whatever had gotten him sad seemed to have gone away, and my tail thumped in appreciation. If Henry was happy, I was happy.

I dove into the food the second he left and scarfed it down as fast as I could. I then licked the bottom of the bowl because sometimes the peanut butter crumbs stuck there. It was kind of like getting dessert with the meal.

Henry had gone into the back, leaving me in charge. That was part of my job. When the customers came in, it was my duty to greet them. He hadn't turned the sign on the door yet, so there was nobody there. Still, I kept an ear out for trouble— or a nose, as the case may be. If something scorched, I started barking, and sometimes I even got an extra treat. You wouldn't believe how many burnt sugar cookies I got one day. Granted, they were in the garbage, but I got them.

I was just finishing breakfast when I heard a creak. My head came up, ears pricked forward to listen harder. The back door didn't usually open that early in the morning. Henry must be taking out the trash.

The door to the alley was kept locked. I knew this because it led to where the trash cans were located. The alley had a thousand different scents—none of which Henry liked me smelling. It was too bad too, because I swore the entire town could be inhaled in that alley.

Footsteps, then Henry cried out in surprise. I pricked my ears, concerned. Was he upset again? Hurt? He usually shouted like that when he chopped his finger or slammed it in the glass case.

I gave a short bark but got no reply, so I pawed at the dividing door. There was a loud thump as something hit the floor. Hard. It reverberated through my paws. I whined, genuinely worried now. I was, after all, head of security, and if my human was in trouble, I needed to save him.

I barked again but got no response. Then, I heard normal baking sounds resume. The mixer came on. Henry must have dropped something, that's all. I stopped whining, satisfied, and settled down for my post-breakfast nap.

The oven door opened as Henry popped something inside. I could only imagine the wonderful things in there. Peanut Butter Twists? Cookies?

I was dreaming about tucking into a bowlful of delicious pastries. The smell was heaven. Sweet, sugary, with nutty over-tones. The scent got stronger... and stronger. It turned acrid, sooty. Huh?

I opened my eyes. That wasn't right. Henry didn't burn things.

Scrambling to my feet, I pawed at the door. Henry relied on me as a backup. Often he'd pat my head and give me a treat for smelling when something was about to burn, and I was getting that feeling now. Big time.

The problem was, there was that darn door between us. Henry didn't like it when I pawed at the door, but I figured under the circumstances he wouldn't mind.

But he didn't come and open it.

I clawed harder, whining louder.

The burning smell seeped under the door. I began to panic. I started barking, but he still didn't come.

Why couldn't I hear his plodding human footsteps?

Henry, where are you?

Frantic now, I raised onto my hind legs and clawed harder. I would dig a hole through that blasted door if I had to. My front paw caught on the silver bar halfway up the door and pulled it down. The door opened.

Ah, so that was the trick. Good to know.

Then all thoughts fled from my mind as I saw Henry. He was lying on the floor.

No.

No.

No.

There was another smell now. More ominous. It was freaking me out. There were spices and flours and sugars and all sorts of different good smells, so it took me a while to figure out what the bad smell was.

I needed to wake Henry and get him to help me figure things out. Besides, he shouldn't have been sleeping then—not there. This was just wrong somehow.

I stuck my nose in his ear and darted my tongue over the earlobe. That usually made him squirm. Only, there was no reaction at all. I rested my paw on his shoulder, but he didn't even look at me.

Henry, wake up!

I growled, low in my throat, my tail tucked between my legs. I didn't like this. Why wasn't he moving?

I circled him, and my paw came down in something wet. Something sticky. Something copper and metallic. Under the scent of all the sugars and spices and flours and creams... I knew this smell. Blood. Henry's blood.

I whined, pawing harder at Henry. I clawed his shoulder. Licked his face.

Who's a good boy? Ask me who's a good boy, Henry.

I looked into his face, but Henry wasn't sleeping. He was gone.

The human on the floor looked like Henry, smelled like Henry, but I could tell Henry wasn't there.

I whined sorrowfully. Henry would never look at me again. He would never ask me if I was a good boy and scratch my ears.

I felt the cool air and looked up. The back door was open, but the alley was empty. There were too many smells to choose what or who might have been there.

I barked, which turned into a cry and then somehow into a howl. Who did this? Where were they? I needed their scent. I needed to find them.

But I couldn't leave. I threw myself down next to my Henry.

What could I do?

Nothing came to mind, so I whined and stared at the open door. I had to find someone to fix this. To bring Henry back. I nudged my human with my nose one last time. When he didn't move, I got to my paws. Then, howling, I ran out into the alley.

Chapter 3

A Very Bad Start To The Day

I was early.

It was one of those perfect days on the cusp of summer when the sun had been up a while, but it still felt as though the day was brand new. I'd be eager to come into work on days like this, just to breathe in the sunshine and feel the cool breeze on my face.

Mostly because I knew it was going to be warm by midday, and right then everything was utterly perfect. Just a little chill —but that just made the coffee feel that much better when I was holding the mug in my hands.

I only needed to get in the door so I could brew that first cup.

The bell above the door jingled as I walked in, and I exhaled, letting the calm of the place settle over me like a favorite quilt.

The shop still smelled faintly of yesterday's peanut butter

twists and roasted beans. I clicked on the overhead pendant lights one by one and then started up the soft jazz playlist I kept queued for the mornings. A few piano notes drifted out of the speakers, bouncing gently off the wooden shelves and rows of books.

I moved through the space, straightening a book here, fluffing a pillow there. The little coffee corner, complete with round tables, mismatched chairs, and a few trailing ivy plants, looked like something out of a lifestyle blog. That alone was a minor miracle, considering what the place looked like when I bought it.

When I drove up here back in January, I was surprised by how much I wanted the dusty old bookstore, so forlorn and neglected. It was something once, but in that first glance it didn't seem like much. Dusty shelves. Tattered paperbacks. Hardbacks with covers half off. The store was already decimated, the "good" stock sold to another store in a neighboring town. I was misled. The advertisement promised a turnkey opportunity.

Instead, it was hard work.

It took six months to clean off the shelves, to rebuild, to restock. To create a space for the coffee counter and decide just where each display would stand.

That day, as I gazed around at the realization of that dream, a soul-deep satisfaction filled me. My footsteps rang on the refinished wooden floors, original to the building, which was over a hundred years old. The wooden shelves along the wall had been polished recently and were now gleaming, with books and games and literary knickknacks arranged in tasteful displays.

The reading alcoves adorned with potted ferns, the seating area by the coffee counter with small round tables ringed by the chairs we used for last night's signing... It was all perfect.

It was easily half an hour before Luke got here. He worked

most days, between classes up at the college, but I was glad I was in a position to offer him flexible hours. He was that good.

Not that I was alone for long. I glanced at the time on my phone. Nearly eight-thirty. Henry should be here soon with the morning pastry delivery. It was midweek, but I expected a smattering of students to be drifting in. The Book Mark had a pretty nice area for studying when it wasn't all set up for events like last night. With finals around the corner, we should be packed. There was going to be a lot of call for that basket of muffins I knew he was probably just taking out of the oven. And his peanut butter twists would see those students through their next study session.

I smiled to myself. Yes, it was going to be a good day.

Instrumental piano continued to float out through hidden Bluetooth speakers as I slipped over to the coffee machine to start a brew for the dispensers we kept at the end of the counter. The regular coffee was free, dark roast. One selection of something a little fun—today's choice involved Michigan cherries. Anything fancier could be purchased along with the pastries, which should be here any minute.

I carried on through the store, sipping my coffee—I liked it black first thing in the morning. More from habit than anything. There was a time I lived off this stuff, but I was working longer hours then, starting my day earlier.

Working too late.

Still, the bitterness on my tongue signaled my brain the day had officially begun as I drifted past the shelves. Adjusting another book. Rearranging the puppet display in the children's area. Making sure there were extra copies right next to the register of the mystery our book club was reading.

Half past.

Henry still wasn't here.

I shot a concerned glance out the window. Maybe he was running late. I hoped he wasn't sick. If he wasn't here in fifteen minutes, I would go over there and pick them up. The bakery opened at nine, like most of us on Main Street, but knowing Henry, he'd already been there for hours, baking.

I was still staring out onto the street when I saw a dark flash run past the front of the store. A black dog. I stared at it, confused. Was that Cocoa?

He turned around and charged back again, tongue hanging out, a wild look in his eyes. Why was Cocoa out in front of my store all by himself?

I knew the dog was pretty good about staying with Henry, so he was rarely on a leash, but I was concerned. He wasn't acting right. He was running in circles, tail down between his legs like he was scared. And he was howling.

Howling.

Something definitely wasn't right.

I opened the front door and stepped outside. The dog was still running up and down the street. By the time I got the door open, he was almost to the bank. I'd started after him when I noticed the pawprints on the pavement.

Red pawprints. Bloody.

My breath caught. Oh, no! The dog was hurt.

And he was clearly scared, judging by his frantic behavior.

I flew down the street after him. "Cocoa! Come here, boy. Good boy. Who's a good boy? Come on, don't run. Cocoa!"

The dog heard me. Stopped. His head was down, ears back, and he was whining.

I slowed down, unsure what to do. I'd heard that injured animals could become vicious in an instant, and I'd never had a pet.

I wished Henry was here. He knew dogs.

Except... where the hell was Henry?

I dropped down into a crouched position and lowered my voice. "Cocoa. Cocoa, come here, boy..."

He must have gotten out. Maybe he'd been hit by a car or

something. Although at first glance, he didn't appear to be limping, and I couldn't see any blood on his fur other than his paws.

I stretched my hands out, calling to him, willing him to come to me.

He did. Stiff-legged and terrified.

Then, he recognized me.

I reached for him as he lunged. The next thing I knew, my arms were full of wriggly dog, whining and crying for all he was worth. I swore he was trying to tell me something.

"Where are you hurt, boy? What happened to you?"

I ran my hands over his body but couldn't find any injury. Yet, there was something very wrong because he was still crying. I'd never heard a dog whine like this before. It was heart-wrenching.

"Where's Henry, boy?"

The dog looked forlornly back at the bakery.

My hand tightened on his collar. "He's inside?"

There were some early shoppers on the street now, and I'd left my store unlocked, but I didn't care. Something hit me in the pit of my stomach, a lump of fear that made the coffee I drank rise like acid into my mouth.

A woman walked past; I recognized her. It was Sophie from the French patisserie.

"Here, take him," I said, shoving the dog at her as she came up the sidewalk.

She reached down to hold Cocoa's collar. "What? Why?"

But I was already running, my feet slapping the pavement. I tore past my own store and tried to open the front door of the bakery. It was locked, and I rebounded backwards.

Something wasn't right. There should be some activity inside the bakery by now. Even with half an hour till opening.

Pawprints. I saw the bloody pawprints on the sidewalk.

Gulping, I followed them around the corner of the building, down the alley, and to the back door that led to the kitchen.

A tendril of smoke snaked out the open door, carrying with it an acrid tang of burning peanut butter.

I pushed open the door and stepped inside. My eyes were immediately drawn to the prone figure on the floor.

No!

A sob welled up in my throat, choking me.

"Henry!"

He was lying on the floor, face down, and there was a black-handled kitchen knife sticking out of his back.

Chapter 4

No One Was Putting Cocoa In The Pound

My hands wouldn't stop shaking.

The 911 call was already a blur. My voice sounded distant, like I was listening to someone else speak. I kept trying to stay calm, trying not to say blood too many times, but I knew I was babbling. There was so much blood.

It was the longest seven minutes of my life. The operator stayed with me, a calm voice in the chaos. I remembered the soft instructions, firm without being commanding. Telling me to do things. I don't even remember what now.

Check for a pulse. She wanted me to check for a pulse. I could still see blood under my fingernails.

By the time the sheriff's cruiser pulled up, lights flashing like a disco party, I had already stepped outside to breathe. Quite a crowd of onlookers had gathered to find out what the commotion was. Sirens and flashing lights were rare for Maple Ridge.

Cocoa hadn't moved from Henry's side. He had dragged Sophie down the alley to the kitchen door, and while she stood pale and shocked out front, he darted in, sniffed Henry's body, and promptly lay down with his head on Henry's foot. I didn't have the heart to pull him away.

The sheriff climbed out of his car with a long-suffering sigh, squinting at the bakery like this was all a huge inconvenience. He looked to be in his mid-sixties, gray at the temples, a slight stoop to his shoulders. His badge read Sheriff Elmer Grady, and he had the energy of someone who had been phasing into retirement since 2017.

"What've we got?" He tugged on a pair of gloves like he was about to weed a flower bed, not walk into a crime scene.

"It's Henry, he's… he's dead." I burst into a sob, my hand covering my mouth. I nodded to the front entrance that was now standing open. I came out this way rather than walk through the smelly alley.

Grady made a face. "Henry? Well, hell. Was just talking to him last week. Something about his rye recipe."

He ambled inside. I followed, not wanting to leave Cocoa alone too long, and watched as the sheriff surveyed the kitchen with a kind of distracted disappointment.

His gaze landed on the tray of peanut butter twists on the counter. "You take those out?"

I nodded. "They were burning, so I took them out while I was… waiting."

He walked over and glanced down at the tray. "What are they?"

I frowned. "Does it matter?"

"It does to me."

I shook my head. "They're peanut butter twists. Henry was famous for them."

"Shame." He sniffed them, pursed his lips, then moved away from the counter. I couldn't see what the peanut butter twists had to do with anything, but the sheriff seemed strangely preoccupied with them. Maybe he was hungry.

"Explain to me how you came to be here?" he said, taking out a notepad and pen, then turning to the front page. It looked brand new.

"I was just setting up when I noticed the dog running up and down the street barking."

"What time was that?"

"Around eight-thirty. I was waiting for Henry to bring the morning order round." I gestured to the burned pastries cooling on the countertop. "Anyway, I went out and saw the bloody pawprints. After I managed to calm the dog down, I went to check on Henry. That's when I found him."

"With the knife in his back?"

I squeezed my eyes shut. "Yes, exactly as he is." I didn't want to look at him anymore. Didn't want to see... this.

The whole thing was a nightmare. A deputy arrived, younger than the sheriff, and walked into the kitchen. "Lindy Huang's on her way, sir."

The sheriff nodded. "Good. Hopefully she can make some sense of all this."

All this? I felt my blood pressure rise. How dare they be so glib about Henry's murder. My friend was lying there with a knife in his back, for goodness' sake. The least they could do was show a little respect.

The deputy made a move toward Henry's body, but Cocoa growled, loud and long, until he stumbled back again.

Good for you, Cocoa, I found myself thinking.

"Can we get this dog out of here?" barked the sheriff. "It's sitting in the middle of a crime scene."

The deputy didn't move.

"He's traumatized," I snapped, my patience wearing thin. "He loved Henry."

"Well, somebody better remove him," the sheriff barked. "Or I'm going to have to call the pound."

No one was putting Cocoa in the pound. Not on my watch. I'd had enough of this guy anyway.

"I'll be next door at the bookstore if you need me," I said, before grabbing a handful of the peanut butter twists.

"Come on, Cocoa. There's a good boy."

My voice was cracking, but I couldn't let my own emotions swamp me right then. Not when that dog needed me.

He'd stopped growling but was watching me. Uncertain. Whining. I extended a hand. "It's your favorite treat."

At first the sorrowful Lab didn't budge, just gazed up at me through those mournful eyes of his, but then his snout was in my hand. While grief-stricken, he wasn't above eating the entire twist in one gulp, burnt or not. I noticed he had blood on his fur now, not just his feet, and he smudged it across the floor as he got up.

I thought the sheriff was going to object, but then he nodded. "I'll be around to talk to you next. Make sure you stay there."

"I'm not going anywhere," I snapped, before walking out and dragging the dog behind me. The crowd had grown, and I saw Gina, the friendly optician, standing with a much-recovered Sophie, who was whispering to her in an animated fashion. No doubt she was describing how we'd found Henry.

Luke stood outside the bookstore, arms crossed, a worried expression on his face. He shook his head when he saw me. "Thank goodness, I was getting worried. Are you okay?"

"I am," I said with a weak nod. "But he's not."

Luke glanced down at the dog, who was shaking violently. Maybe it was shock, or maybe fear, I wasn't sure. He was in new surroundings, having lost the only person who cared for him. It was no wonder he was trembling.

"Bring him inside," Luke said. "Let's get him away from all these people."

I followed him in, dragging Cocoa with me. The blood on his paws had dried now, and his tail was firmly between his legs.

"Poor thing's terrified," I murmured, releasing his collar and instead stroking his head. He sat down with a whine.

Luke poured some water into a bowl and laid it at Cocoa's feet. He studied it for a long moment, then sniffed it before starting to lap it up thirstily.

"What happened?" Luke asked once I had taken a seat at the coffee counter. "Is Henry really dead?"

I gave a grim nod. "Cocoa was going mental on the street outside, so I went to check on Henry and found him lying on the floor." I told him about the knife in his back. "It must have hit an artery or something because there was a puddle of blood underneath him." I shuddered. "It was horrible."

The coffee machine was gurgling, and I realized Luke was making me a warm drink. A hot chocolate landed on the bar in front of me.

"Here," he said. "Drink this. It'll help with the shock."

I wrapped my hands around it. The heat was comforting, even just to hold. "Who would want to kill Henry?" I whispered. "He was so nice."

Luke gave a sad nod. "I don't know. Someone, obviously."

"The sheriff's there now, but he doesn't look too competent. I hope he'll be able to figure out who did this."

"I doubt it," Luke said. "The only crime fighting Elmer Grady ever does is haul in drunk college students and break up frat parties. This is way out of his league."

I stared at him, horrified. "So who's going to solve Henry's murder, then?"

"They'll probably bring someone in from outside," came a

voice at the entrance. I glanced up as Gina walked in. "I'm so sorry to hear about Henry. He was such a nice man."

"I know." I couldn't stop my eyes from filling with tears. To hide my emotions, I took a gulp of hot chocolate.

Gina reached down and patted Cocoa on the head. The dog had curled up at my feet, under the coffee bar counter. "Who did this to your master, eh?"

The dog whined in response.

"Speak of the devil," muttered Luke as the door opened again and Sheriff Grady walked in.

"I'd like to ask you some more questions, young lady," he said, coming to stand at the bar beside me, notebook still in hand. I saw he had made a half-page of notes. Not much for a crime scene like that. This did not restore my faith in him.

"My name is Tess Holloway," I gritted out. "In case you were wondering."

He dutifully made a note in his book. I met Luke's gaze and rolled my eyes. Gina was still standing on the other side of me, leaning on the counter.

"Run me through what happened this morning. After you entered the kitchen and found Henry Dawson on the floor, what did you do next?"

"I called 911."

"But you took those pastries out of the oven."

What was it with those damn peanut butter twists?

"Yes, but I called 911 first. The operator told me to check Henry's pulse to see if he was still alive." I gulped, staring down at my hands. "He wasn't. That's when I crossed to the oven and took out the pastries. They were smoking up the kitchen."

"Did you do anything else?"

"Cocoa came running in. Sophie had let him loose, and he—"

"Sophie?"

"Sophie Beaumont. I asked her to keep hold of the dog because he was going crazy outside."

The sheriff made another note. "What then?"

"Then I went out for some air. I didn't want to... I couldn't look at him anymore." I shook my head as the vision of Henry on the floor flashed behind my eyes. "That's when you drove up."

"Was the front door locked when you got there?" he asked.

My eyebrows lifted. Maybe he wasn't a total idiot after all.

"Yes. I went in the back door, which was ajar. Henry hadn't opened up shop yet. He normally opened at nine."

"So you unlocked it?"

"Yes, I went out that way to wait for you."

He wrote something else in his notebook, his hand moving slowly across the page. Sheriff Grady wasn't a fast writer. I thought I knew what it was—the killer had to have come in the back. That much was obvious.

"And you didn't see anything unusual when you got there?" Grady asked.

I shook my head. "I was too shocked by Henry to notice anything else."

"You said the back door was open." He scowled at me like it was my fault.

"Yes, I ran straight in."

"It hadn't been tampered with?"

"I don't know. I didn't look."

The way he was gazing at me made me feel uncomfortable. "Is that blood on your hands?"

I clenched my fists. "I felt Henry's pulse, like the 911 operator told me to do."

"We'll have to take a sample," he said. "If you'll come with me next door. Our forensic lady is there now."

"Lindy Huang," Luke confirmed, using her full name.

I raised an eyebrow. "Lindy works for the sheriff's office?"

"She is a forensics professor," he said with a proud nod.

That made sense. This was a small town, with an even smaller sheriff's department. It tracked that they used a college scientist for their forensic work, since it probably wasn't often they had any.

"Sheriff, you can't seriously think Tess had anything to do with Henry's murder?" Gina was saying, staring across at the big man whose stomach was stretching his khaki button-down shirt to its limits.

"She was the first person at the crime scene."

"So?" Luke and I said at the same time.

"She has the victim's blood on her hands."

"Literally, not figuratively," I said, but that was lost on him.

"Now, please, Miss Holloway."

I glanced at Luke and Gina as I got up to follow him outside. This was just great. Not only was I traumatized by my friend's murder, having found his body, but now, somehow, I had become a suspect.

Chapter 5

A Motive For Murder?

"What I want to know is why Cocoa didn't attack the murderer," Luke said once I got back. "I mean, he was always with Henry."

Lindy was lovely as she took my fingerprints and a quick swab of the blood under my fingernails before sending me on my way. "It's just to rule you out," she said as she packaged up my samples.

I purposely ignored the sheriff as I stomped back to the bookstore.

"I don't think Henry had him in the kitchen when he was baking," Gina offered. "Food hygiene and all that."

"Makes sense." I thought for a moment. "You know, there were scratch marks on the door leading from the front area to the kitchen. I noticed when we went back inside. That must have been Cocoa trying to get in." Cocoa glanced up, whimpered, and then put his head back down again. I took that as an affirmative. "Still, with the front door locked, he must have managed somehow, because he escaped that way into the alley. It was just too late."

"Clever boy," Gina said, stroking him. "You went to get help."

"We were all too late," I added with a sigh.

Luke shook his head. "A knife in the back. That sounds personal to me. Who do we know who has a beef with Henry?"

We all looked at each other.

"Sophie Beaumont," I whispered, saying what we were all thinking. "I heard them arguing last night."

"We all did," Gina confirmed. "But that doesn't mean she killed him.".

"No, but it might give her a motive," Luke said. He sounded so professional for his young age, and then I remembered he was studying criminology.

"Why were they arguing?" I struggled to remember through the fog in my mind. Over the last few hours, a heavy cloud had descended, and I couldn't shake it.

"Henry said she was always trying to show him up," Luke pointed out.

"Oh yes, I remember now. Never misses an opportunity to outdo him, that's what he said."

"Hardly motive for murder," Gina mused.

"I couldn't imagine anyone wanting to kill Henry," I murmured. "He was the sweetest man in Maple Ridge."

My first friend. I still remembered how we met. He came around and brought a box of freshly baked peanut butter twists to the store to welcome me, Cocoa by his side.

"Where's Suzanne?" I asked, jumping off my chair so fast that Cocoa growled.

"Who?" Gina asked.

"Henry's shop assistant. She helps with the morning rush.

I'm pretty sure she usually gets there around eight-thirty to help him open up, but she didn't this morning."

"The police were there. Maybe she was frightened," Gina suggested.

"Still, if your boss had just been murdered, you'd go in and see what had happened, wouldn't you?" I looked at each of them. "I mean, I would."

Luke nodded. "The sheriff must know Henry had an assistant."

"He didn't ask," I muttered. "Unless someone tells him, he's not going to know."

Gina straightened up. "I'll do it. I was about to head back anyway. Tess, I'll pop in after work and see how you're getting on." She rubbed me kindly on the back. It was a simple gesture, but I appreciated it more than she knew. I was one cross word away from bursting into tears. Honestly, the hot chocolate was the only thing holding me together.

That and the dog's furry presence at my feet.

"Thanks, Gina."

I drained the rest of my now not-hot chocolate and set the mug down on the bar counter. "You know, I took a look at that kitchen door when I went back there," I told Luke. "It hadn't been forced. There wasn't a scratch on it."

"That's strange," Luke mused. "It must mean that Henry left the door unlocked while he was baking."

"Or he let the killer in," I finished.

Luke stared at me. "That means Henry may have known his killer!"

I nodded, and we contemplated this in silence for a moment. Was it someone we knew? Part of our community? At my feet, Cocoa gave a little grunt, his eyes closed. I wished I could just go to sleep and block out the world like that. Not happening today, though.

A customer came into the bookstore and I went to serve

her while Luke loaded our mugs into the dishwasher. I instantly recognized her as one half of the couple from last night. Carly, wasn't it?

"Hello again." My voice was shaky, so I cleared my throat. "Nice to see you."

"Oh, Tess. I was so sorry to hear about Henry. What a shock for you too."

Crumbs, it had just happened and the whole town already knew about it—and that I found his body. I hoped Carly hadn't come here to gossip. I really wasn't in the mood.

"Thank you." I didn't say anything else, not wanting to encourage her.

"Anyway, that's not why I came by," she said, turning to the display. "I'm desperate to get my hands on the latest Sally Westcombe. I saw you had it in stock last night."

I exhaled, relieved. Sally Westcombe's romantic fantasy series was all over BookTok.

"Sure, no problem." I took one off the display and handed it to her. She stroked it like it was something sacred. It had a beautiful cover, dark purple with gold foiling, intricate details, and a smooth sheen. Carly was a fellow book lover.

I warmed to her. "If you like Sally's books, you might enjoy these too."

I led her over to a bookshelf behind a round table with a vase of flowers on it. Sunlight streamed in the window and bounced off the polished surface. It had warmed up, just like I knew it would, but my day was anything but perfect now.

Carly studied the book I gave her and read the blurb on the back cover, then she nodded. "You're right. I'll take them both."

I managed a weak smile. "Excellent. I think you'll really enjoy them."

We went over to the till. "You're not at work today?" I asked, as she took out her wallet.

"Not till later. Most of my classes are in the afternoon, which suits me perfectly. I like waking up a little later, then messing around in my studio before I have to prepare for my lessons."

I'd forgotten she'd said she was an art teacher. "So you paint too?" It seemed like a dumb question, but she didn't say as much. Her grin just widened. "Yes, I got my degree in fine art. You should come round sometime, I'll show you the gallery."

"The gallery?"

"Yes, my husband and I run a gallery at the east end of Maple Street. We're not always there, but it's our pride and joy."

I felt myself relaxing. "I'd love to."

Everyone was so nice here. Well, almost everyone. I spotted Sophie Beaumont walk past the shop window and frowned. She was up early this morning. As far as I knew, her store also opened at nine, so it was strange she was outside Henry's bakery half an hour before when she would have also have had to prep.

I didn't have time to dwell on it because the bells at the front of the store jangled as another customer came in, a student judging by the loose-fitting jeans, the casual shirt, and the backpack slung low over one shoulder. I said goodbye to Carly and went to see if I could help.

Cocoa was now sniffing around the store, poking his nose into all the corners, probably hoping to find some crumbs he could scarf up. I wondered if he'd had anything to eat other than the peanut butter twists I fed him this morning in an attempt to get him to leave the bakery.

It turned out all the student wanted was a black coffee and a quiet place to study, so I left him to Luke and stepped outside again. Sophie was gone, so I turned toward the bakery, where the two sheriff's vehicles had been joined by an ambulance, a station wagon I recognized as Lindy's car, and a sleek, black SUV.

The road had been cordoned off by bright yellow sheriff's tape that fluttered in the breeze, and the traffic had been rerouted. It didn't stop the stream of pedestrians, though, who came to find out what was going on and to gawk at the crime scene. The crime rate, I'd heard, was very low in Maple Ridge, so this was something of an anomaly.

As I watched, the ambulance drove off, probably taking Henry's body away, and Lindy came out of the bakery accompanied by a tall, serious-faced man with broad shoulders, brown hair, and a square jaw. He wore black suit pants with a crisp white shirt, which I had to admit fit him very well. No tie, no jacket. From the way he was standing, arms folded, nodding as he listened to what she was saying, he made me think he was someone important. Or at least professional, not like the bumbling, pastry-obsessed Sheriff Grady.

Maybe there was hope that justice would prevail, after all.

The man looked up and caught my eye. I quickly turned and headed back into the bookstore. No way was I being drawn back in for more questioning. Not right then, anyway. I was exhausted, spent, emotionally drained, and it wasn't even noon yet.

Unfortunately, my day wasn't going to get any better.

Chapter 6

Comfort Chicken

I walked in to find Cocoa waiting anxiously for me inside the doorway as if asking if there was any news. He had a stuffed chicken in his mouth from the farm display I'd set up in the children's area.

I started to protest then stopped. Let him have it. The poor dog had lost everything else.

I scratched his ears, and he pawed at my leg. I looked down and noticed the blood. It was crusted around his paws and still on his fur. Maybe it was time I did something about that.

Washing a black Lab in a small store bathroom was every bit as impossible as you might imagine. I used a ton of soap, but I still couldn't get all the blood out. This dog needed a visit to a dog groomer, and I didn't even know where one was.

Finally, I gave up and rinsed his paws in the bowl of water I'd poured from the basin and put on the floor. Somehow, I managed to get more soapsuds on me than the dog. Using a rag, I washed the blood from his undercarriage. Unimpressed, Cocoa gave a shake, his long tail smacking against the door.

It opened and Luke peered in. "You managing okay?"

Cocoa bolted from the room, skidding across the wooden floor toward the entrance. "Oops, I'll get him."

Luke left me there and thundered after the dog. I looked around at the mess that was the bathroom and sighed. It was utter chaos. Water splashed across the floor, soapy foam everywhere but mostly on me, and now a wet dog on the loose in the bookstore.

I heard a customer scream and got to my feet. This mess would have to wait. Toweling myself off, I stared at my bedraggled reflection in the mirror and shuddered. Good heavens, what would my customers say?

I straightened my hair, running a brush I kept in the bathroom cabinet through it, flattened my blouse and tucked it into my skirt, then wiped away a smear of dirt on my cheek. Where had that come from? At least the blood had come out from underneath my fingernails.

When I ventured out, Luke had managed to get the dog under control, but the vase of flowers on the corner table had been knocked over. Thankfully there hadn't been much water in it, but even so, there was a small puddle and the flowers were scattered all over the floor.

I had just finished cleaning up when the bell jingled and Lindy walked in. She had changed out of her forensic suit and wore a pair of jeans and a pretty blouse with tiny pink flowers on it.

Luke greeted her and, after sitting Cocoa—who had found his chicken and was holding on to it as if it was his only friend—at his feet behind the counter, set about making her a coffee.

"Lindy, hey," I said, wiping my hands on the cloth I was holding. "How'd it go?"

"Awful seeing him like that," she said, shaking her head. Henry had been a stalwart figure in the small town, important in his own right.

I nodded, the ache in my heart still there.

"Did you find any prints on the knife?" Luke asked as the coffee machine coughed and spluttered. "Any trace DNA left behind?"

She smiled at her student. "I can't talk about an active case, you know that."

"Aw, come on," he moaned, setting the foamiest cappuccino in front of her—with chocolate sprinkles. "I'm trying to learn here."

"What can you tell us?" I asked, trying to get her to open up.

She hesitated, then said, "Well, as you know, Henry was stabbed from behind."

I swallowed, not wanting to go back there in my mind, but the image came anyway. Henry, lying on the floor... blood everywhere... the black knife sticking out of his back.

"It was right in the middle of his back," I said.

"Pierced his heart," she confirmed. "Severed the aorta. That's why there was so much blood."

I felt sick, but Luke was staring at her, riveted. "So the murderer had medical knowledge?"

She shrugged. "Or they just got lucky."

Not so lucky for Henry. From behind the counter, I heard Cocoa whimper.

"He may not even have seen his attacker," I said, frowning at the thought of someone sneaking up on Henry.

"Impossible to say," Lindy corrected. "They could have had an altercation, during which Henry turned his back on them."

"Then they picked up the knife and stabbed him," finished Luke.

I drew in a breath, then it struck me. "It was a black-handled knife, right?" I looked at Lindy.

She nodded. "So?"

"How do we know it was one of Henry's?"

"Good point," Luke said, his eyes wide. "We need to take a look in Henry's kitchen and see what knives he used."

"That's not conclusive," Lindy told us. "We'd never know for sure if it belonged to Henry. I will, of course, test it for fingerprints. That will tell us if Henry had used it or not."

I nodded. That would be good enough.

"How's Cocoa holding up?" Lindy asked.

"Not well. At the moment he's living on peanut butter twists and water. We have to get him some proper dog food."

"The grocery store at the end of Pine Avenue will have kibble," Lindy said.

"I'll go after work." It was a couple miles' walk to the store, and I couldn't leave the bookstore for that long.

"I'll cycle down for you," Luke offered. I shot him a grateful smile.

"Thanks, Luke. That would be great."

"Pity we don't have a lead for Cocoa, or I could take him with."

I frowned. "The lead must be at the bakery. I didn't think to look for it when I was there."

"It's a crime scene now," Lindy said. "Off limits, I'm afraid. Even I'm not allowed back in without special permission from the detective in charge."

"Detective?" Luke and I said simultaneously.

"Was that the man you were speaking to outside the bakery earlier?" I asked Lindy.

She gave a tight nod. "Detective Larsen Maddox. He's here from Boston to oversee the investigation."

Thank goodness for that.

"I'm sure he'll want to speak to you," Lindy pointed out. "Once he's done at the crime scene."

I shuddered at the thought of more questioning. "I'll be here," I said, but there was an edge to my voice.

"The samples I took will clear you from any wrongdoing," Lindy assured me. "He'll just want to know how you came to discover Henry's body."

That made sense, although it didn't make me feel any better. Lindy finished her coffee and left as more customers came in. I didn't have the energy to see to them, so I sat behind the coffee machine with Cocoa and his chicken while Luke took care of them.

Then he went to get dog food, and for the first time that day, I was alone.

Chapter 7

For My Sins

I sat at one of the tables near the front window, mug clutched in both hands. Cocoa lay beneath my chair, his chin resting on his paws, eyes tracking every movement like he was still waiting for Henry to walk through the door and fix this whole mess.

Except he wasn't going to.

The chime over the door jingled, but this time, it wasn't a customer. It was the Boston detective—what was his name again? Maddox? He moved with clipped purpose, his gaze sweeping the shop once before landing on me.

I realized he probably wasn't much older than me—mid-thirties, maybe forty at most. Threads of gray had begun to weave through his dark hair, giving it a salt-and-pepper look that hadn't fully taken hold yet. His face was square but not heavy, like it had been carved with purpose. There were the early traces of lines, etched by experience rather than age.

Clean-shaven, his jaw was strong, the set of it suggesting someone who had made a habit of taking life seriously.

I could tell by the scowl that he wasn't happy to be here.

Cocoa glanced up, eyed the detective, then put his head back down next to the stuffed chicken. I was surprised. Usually he was more protective than that. Maybe he was also worn out after the events of the day. Or maybe he sensed the detective wasn't a threat.

Either way, I didn't have the same luxury.

Limbs complaining, I pushed myself out of the chair. "Can I help you?" Even though I knew exactly who he was.

"Detective Maddox from Boston PD. I'm in charge of the homicide investigation. I believe you're Tess Holloway?"

I nodded, still feeling shaky. "For my sins."

He frowned. "What sins?"

"Nothing, I didn't mean... Never mind." I gulped. This was not going well. "Yes, I'm Tess."

He came further into the store. "You found the victim this morning?"

"I did." I walked over to the coffee bar and slid onto a stool, gesturing for him to do the same. He shook his head and remained standing.

Fine, be like that. I needed to sit.

"Could you talk me through what happened?"

I sighed. "I've already been through this with Sheriff Grady."

"I'd like you to go through it again—with me." His voice was deep enough to send shivers down my spine.

So I started again, from the beginning. How I had come in early to get a jump on the day, seen the dog going crazy outside, left him with Sophie, and gone to check on Henry. I gave him Sophie's details, just like I had with Grady.

"What did you do once you were inside the bakery?" Those dark eyes seemed to be staring right through me. I shifted on the stool, casting my mind back to that horrible moment.

"I called 911 and spoke to the operator, who told me to check Henry's pulse. I did, but he was already dead." The knife and inordinate amount of blood kind of gave that away.

"Then I took the peanut butter twists out of the oven because they were burning, and Cocoa ran in."

"Cocoa?"

"Henry's dog. The one that was going crazy outside my window this morning."

Hearing his name, Cocoa picked up his chicken and strolled over from his spot under the table. He stopped at my feet and looked up at me as if to say, "You called?"

I bent down and fondled his ears. "I think he was trying to get help."

Hot tears pricked my eyelids, and I blinked rapidly. I was not going to cry in front of this big, mean Boston detective.

"How well did you know the victim?"

"His name's Henry," I muttered, shooting him an annoyed look. I was not going to think about him as the victim. "And I knew him relatively well. I was one of his customers, and his friend."

"How long have you been friends?"

"Since I arrived in Maple Ridge six months ago." I blinked again, more rapidly.

He considered this for a moment, then sighed. "Do you know of anyone who would want to harm Henry?" I was pleased he had used his name. They might all just be victims at Boston PD, but here we still showed a little respect.

"I honestly don't. He was the sweetest guy. Everybody loved him."

"Not everybody," Maddox murmured.

I bit my lip. No, clearly not everyone.

Then I remembered the party. My face must have given it away because he said, "What?"

"Nothing."

"What were you thinking just then?"

Darn, he was good.

"Oh, it's nothing relevant to the case but..." I stopped, unsure whether to continue. My discussion with Gina and Luke came back to me. It wasn't a motive for murder.

"But?" he prompted.

I sighed. "I had an author signing event here last night. Several of the local business owners came, and I overheard Henry arguing with Sophie Beaumont. She owns the French patisserie a few blocks down."

His expression was unreadable. "What were they arguing about?"

"Henry was complaining that she always tries to outdo him," I said.

Maddox frowned. "In what way?"

"They're in direct competition with each other," I explained. "Henry said she always tries to poach his customers. That was it."

He was silent for a beat.

"See, I told you it was nothing." I shouldn't have said anything.

"Sophie Beaumont, the same woman who looked after your dog this morning?"

"He's not my dog, he's Henry's," I corrected. "But yes, I asked her to hold him for me. She was in the street nearby."

"What was she doing there?" He asked the question casually, like it meant nothing, but I knew it was important. Unlike Grady, Maddox was no dummy.

"I don't know. You'll have to ask her that."

He nodded, and pulling his phone out of his back pocket, he made a note. No brand-new notepads for Detective

Maddox. I watched his hands as he typed—long fingers wrapped around the device, his thumbs rapidly working on the screen. He was wearing a weapon. I caught a glimpse of it as he shifted position. A dangerous man.

"Anyone else I should know about?" he asked, glancing around the shop. I saw his gaze settle on the damp spot on the rug underneath the table where the vase had fallen over. He was astute too. Didn't miss much.

"No, like I said, Henry was well liked in the town."

"In that case, I'll leave you be. Have a good afternoon, Miss Holloway." He nodded, spun on his heel, and left the shop. The bell jingled softly behind him, too cheerful for comfort.

I was left staring after him. He might be curt and get straight to the point, but he was professional. Maybe there was some hope after all.

Chapter 8

Early Morning Walks

"Here you go. A nice, new bed." I set the big, fluffy dog bed that Luke had bought for Cocoa down in the living area of my two-bedroom apartment.

I rented the ground floor of a big white clapboard house tucked away at the edge of town. It was one of those old New England builds with a deep front porch, mismatched windows, and a sloping lawn that must be hell to mow.

The upstairs belonged to my landlady, who mostly kept to herself, except when she brought down baked goods or asked for help getting her cat out of a tree.

My place was quiet, a little drafty in the winter, and blessed with tall windows that caught the morning light just right. It wasn't fancy, but it was home. And now it had a dog.

I wondered how the cat would feel about that.

I turned to find Cocoa standing at the front door, staring at me. I patted the bed. "Come on, boy. This is for you."

He didn't move.

Luke had also bought us dog food, a leash, and a large bone for Cocoa to chew on that looked like it was made out of plastic but wasn't. At least I hoped it wasn't.

I tried using food instead. It was nearly six o'clock, and while I wasn't sure if Cocoa'd had breakfast, he'd certainly had his fill of pastries and milk during the course of the day. We'd also used a plastic container as a water bowl, so he'd been okay.

I poured some kibble into the shiny new silver bowl and added some of the dog food from the giant can. It actually didn't smell too bad.

Putting the bowl on the floor, I tried again. "Come on, boy. Supper's ready."

Still no movement. Instead, he lay down on the doorstep and gazed mournfully over at me. My heart broke. The poor thing. Nothing was familiar.

Sighing, I went outside and sat on the doorstep with him. "You miss Henry, eh?"

He gave a soft whine and rested his head on my thigh. I scratched gently behind his ears. He enjoyed that because he inched his head closer.

"I'm sad about Henry too," I said, letting out a breath I didn't know I was holding. "He was a good friend. I'm sure they'll find whoever did this," I continued after a beat. "That Boston detective seems very smart."

Another whine. It was like we were communicating.

"I'm sorry you can't go home," I continued, still scratching. "But this is my house. I'll look after you until..." I faded off. Until what? Until we can find someone to take you?

Cocoa was staring up at me.

"Scratch that," I said. "You can stay with me. Period. I'll look after you." I realized I'd just inherited a dog.

After our little talk, I left Cocoa's food within eyesight and went about my evening, cooking supper, eating at my kitchen table, and then settling down to watch some TV.

I was halfway through the police procedural when I heard snuffling behind me and realized Cocoa had eventually ventured inside and was eating his supper—from his new bowl.

Yes! I was so happy that I waited until he was done and then called him over.

"Good boy, Cocoa. Who's a good boy?"

I opened my arms, and he came flying across the room so fast that I wound up sitting on the floor as sixty pounds of black Lab tried to crawl into my lap, all the while frantically licking every inch of my face he could find.

That dog food didn't smell so good now, I can tell you. Still, this was a good thing, so I hugged him back and tried not to think about the drool on my face.

I moved the bed closer to the sofa, and after I'd sat in it myself and patted the cushion, Cocoa tentatively got in. He walked in a tight circle for five minutes, sniffing every fold in the material, before finally committing and sitting down.

"Thank you," I said, relieved. Maybe this was going to work out after all.

That's how the two of us stayed until I finally turned in, leaving Cocoa in his new bed in the living room.

I woke up to a sharp bark next to my ear and felt warm breath in my face.

"What—?"

Opening my eyes, I saw a wet snout and two dark, hairy eyes staring at me.

"Holy crap!" I spluttered and sat up to get away from the monster of my dreams. There was another bark, and my fog lifted, even though my heart was hammering like a freight train.

"Cocoa, oh my gosh. You scared the hell out of me."

He panted and gave a low whine.

"What time is it?" I glanced at my phone beside the bed. Four a.m. "It's the middle of the night, Cocoa. Go back to bed."

But he wouldn't. He sat there and barked until I finally threw back the covers and got up. "What? Do you need to pee? Is that it?"

I stomped down the hall, regretting the moment I'd set eyes on the mutt, and opened the front door. "There. Have at it."

He scampered past me outside, ran around the garden once, and then came back and stared at me as if he expected me to follow.

"I'm not coming out there. It's cold. I want to go back to bed." It was dark too. The sun wasn't even up, and it was midsummer. Madness, that's what this was.

"Are you coming inside or what?"

Cocoa stared defiantly back at me, then barked some more.

"Hush," I hissed. "You'll wake my landlady, and she's not going to be too impressed to find you here." I'd have some explaining to do tomorrow. She was an animal lover, thank goodness, so I didn't think it would be a problem, but I'd have to ask permission. If she said no, then I guess we'd both be moving.

He kept barking until I relented. Jeez, this dog really knew how to get his way.

"Okay, okay. I'm coming." If only to shut him up.

"Give me a minute," I said, and leaving the door open, I went back to my bedroom and pulled on some sweatpants and a shirt that was lying around. I was so going back to bed when this was over. I grabbed my tennis shoes and the leash, just in case, and went back outside.

Cocoa was where I'd left him, waiting on the path for me. That was something, I guessed.

We set off toward town. There were plenty of good walks around here, but Cocoa had somewhere particular in mind, so I let him walk and followed behind.

There was a cool breeze, and I was glad for my thick sweatshirt. We kept going until we reached the outskirts of town, and then we turned down a road that I recognized as Henry's.

Cocoa was going home.

"Oh, boy," I said, calling after him. "We can't go in here. It's not allowed." Indeed, as we got closer, I could see the sheriff's tape around the house, blocking off the front door. I wasn't entirely sure why, since Henry had been killed at the bakery, but the police must have wanted to search his house too.

To my surprise, Cocoa didn't stop there. He trotted past and turned down a path that led into a wooded area. I hesitated. It was dark, I didn't have a flashlight, and this dog was leading me into the woods.

This was all kinds of crazy. I should turn around right now and go home.

Yet for some reason, I didn't. Cocoa paused and turned around as if to say, "Are you coming?" His eyes were luminous in the darkness.

"Wait for me, boy," I called as I increased my pace. If we were going to do this, I wanted to stay by his side.

A few moments later, the path ended, and I was standing in a wide, open expanse with a lake in front of me.

"I had no idea this was here," I told Cocoa, pausing to take it in. The oval-shaped lake glistened in the moonlight, its black surface shimmering like polished obsidian. Around it, as far as the eye could see, were trees—pines, firs, and every other kind of tree that grew in these parts. I bet in the fall this was incredible.

"What are we doing here, boy?" I asked, as Cocoa lifted his head and barked at the moonlight. That looked therapeutic. I might try it sometime.

The dog took off again, and I followed. We walked along the south shore, and despite not wanting to come, I had to marvel at the undisturbed beauty of the place. It was dark, but with the moonlight and stars, there was enough light to see by.

It was magical. Like something out of a fairy tale.

Cocoa obviously knew this route because he ran around lifting his leg on several trees, sniffing others, and turning back to check on me every few minutes, his tongue hanging out. He seemed to be in his element.

After ten minutes, the path forked, and Cocoa took the one meandering away from the lake. It cut through some more trees, but I could see wooden cabins with porch lights flickering behind the tree line. A short while later, we emerged onto a residential street, well lit with streetlamps.

I sighed in relief, even though I'd really enjoyed being by the lake.

Cocoa seemed to know exactly where he was going, so I just followed, half intrigued and half enjoying the fresh morning air on my face. After yesterday's experience, it felt like this was lifting my spirits and restoring my soul.

Who knew an early morning walk could be so invigorating?

The streets were more familiar now, and I wasn't surprised when we emerged onto Main Street, a block away from the bakery and my store. As Cocoa came to a stop outside the alley, I finally got it.

"This is the route Henry and you took every morning, isn't it?" I asked him. He panted up at me, his long tongue lolling out of his mouth. "That's why you woke me at four—it's your routine."

Except now we were in the middle of town and a mile away from home. It was Sunday. I wasn't opening the bookstore today. Henry didn't open on Sundays either, but I guess the dog got confused, what with everything that had happened.

Since my bookstore keys were on my key ring along with my house keys, I decided to go in. I could use a glass of water, and Cocoa was panting up at me expectantly.

I poured some water into a bowl and set it on the floor. He dove straight in and began lapping loudly. I drank a glass of water from the tap.

Once we were done, I looked at him, my head tilted to one side. "Cocoa, we have to walk home now. I don't have any food for you here."

He licked his chops and nudged my hand.

"I'm sorry, boy, but we have to go home first. Come on, let's get back and I'll give you some breakfast."

I think he actually understood because he followed me out of the bookstore without a whine or a bark of protest.

Chapter 9

The Cuddling Kind

Cocoa

I waited while Tess opened the door and stepped aside.

"Alright, buddy," she said tiredly. "We're home."

I hesitated. It just didn't smell like home.

It wasn't bad, just different. There was the fresh paint, and I could smell a trace of lemon from something she used for cleaning, maybe pine from the floorboards. But there was no flour. No burnt cookie edges.

No Henry.

"Not this again," Tess begged as she clunked around in the kitchen. My stomach growled. I was pretty darn hungry, and Henry always fed me after a walk. She put my bowl down and stepped aside. "It's there when you want it."

My stomach gave another rumble, so I padded inside.

Breakfast was good, so I wolfed it down in under a minute. Gotta be a new record. As I licked my lips, I thought that Tess bought better dog food than Henry.

Glancing up, I found her watching me, a faint smile on her face. My tail thumped against her leg. She was alright, this one. She was still learning how to be a good human, but she had potential. Her ear scratches weren't bad, even though they were softer than Henry's. She even found the spot Henry always got with his thumb.

Not the same. But not bad.

To my surprise, she didn't make her own breakfast but went back into her bedroom. She must be tired. I conducted another inspection of my own bed. Why'd they make them so fluffy? It's like you're drowning in cushions. I walked over and stepped on it. My paws sank in, so I removed them again. I circled it, then tried lying down again. Too springy.

I stood back up and sniffed in the crevices. No crumbs in the corners. Nothing to snack on if I get hungry in the night. I'd have to remedy that.

My food bowl is kind of cool, though. The first time I looked into it, I saw my own eyes staring back at me. Gave me a shock before I worked out what it was.

Later, after another scratch behind the ears, the house grew quiet. The wind rustled in the trees outside. I lay on the bouncy bed again and tried to settle, but my chest ached. Not the kind of ache you can lick or stretch.

I missed Henry.

I knew he was gone. He smelled... not alive. Like the shell of something instead of the thing itself. Like a toy that doesn't squeak anymore.

I got up and wandered through the apartment. Tess's bedroom door was almost closed. I nudged it open with my nose. It gave way with a soft creak.

She was already asleep, breathing slow and deep. Her hand dangled over the edge of the bed, so I sniffed it and nudged it gently. She didn't stir.

I hoped she wouldn't mind, so I climbed up very carefully,

one paw at a time. She didn't wake. I curled into a ball at her feet, my chin resting on her toes.

Henry wasn't a cuddler. He let me sleep near him some-times, but on the rug by the bed. Tess looked like the cuddling kind. I hoped so.

Her breathing stayed even.

I listened to it, thinking about the walk we'd taken earlier. She was slow, slower than Henry, but she tried. She didn't complain when I led us the long way, back to the start of the route Henry and I used to take. She didn't stop me from peeing on my favorite lamppost either.

That was nonnegotiable. I had to reclaim it. The other dogs needed to know I was still in the game.

She enjoyed the lake, I could tell. That was Henry's favorite spot too. Mine as well, except for that one day. The day the man had been there. The one Henry didn't like.

I remembered how his body changed when he saw him. It grew tight, and he bristled, like I do when I sense danger. I'd never heard Henry growl before, but that day he did, and worse, I'd smelled fear on him.

Tess was worried too. I don't understand the words she says, but I get the message. I hear it in the way her voice catches when she says Henry's name.

And that big man with the badge who came to the bakery —he was scary, yet surprisingly, his smell was calm and controlled. I liked him. He had a good smell.

I hoped he would help us.

I shifted slightly, tail thumping once before I tucked it in.

Tess murmured in her sleep, her foot twitching under my chin.

A surge of something I couldn't explain encompassed me. I'd protect her. Just like Henry.

I closed my eyes, ears twitching at the morning noises outside. Then I fell asleep, wrapped around Tess's feet.

Chapter 10

I'll Get The Goldfish

On Monday morning, I came into the store breathless and late. Apparently, Henry had a rhythm to the day which most sane people didn't have. That dratted dog had woken me up at four in the freaking morning. Again.

"Your cheeks are red," Luke commented as I walked past to dump my backpack in the back office. It was where I did the accounts and other admin tasks for the bookstore.

"I went on a five-mile hike at four o'clock this morning," I said, glaring at Cocoa, who was somehow grinning and holding his chicken in his mouth at the same time.

"For real?" asked Luke.

"No, but close enough." After the lake routine, we staggered home, and like an idiot, I went back to sleep. Hence my tardiness. I never expected having a dog would make things so complicated.

He grinned. "It'll keep you fit."

"I'd rather do it at a normal hour," I grumbled, unlocking the office.

Luke made me a coffee, and I set about neatening the window displays while soft music played in the background. Cocoa had taken up his position on the rug under the table, and I finally felt myself relax.

Life was just beginning to make sense again when the door jangled and a young woman with close-cropped, spiky black hair swept in. Her mascara was smudged, and her nose was red from crying.

My short-lived calm evaporated in a hiss from the coffee machine.

"Suzanne!" I gasped, straightening up so fast I got dizzy. "It's you."

"I heard about Henry. It's too terrible."

I put a hand on her shoulder and led her over to the coffee bar, nodding at Luke to make her something hot and sweet.

"Come and sit down. Why did you come here?"

"Because my optician told me to."

"Gina?" I frowned.

"Yes, I've just been there for my eye test, and she said to come straight here and talk to you. Apparently you were looking for me?"

"Yes, that's right. We thought you'd be working at the bakery on Saturday."

"I usually do work a full day on Saturday, but Henry gave me the day off. I was at a friend's birthday party. I didn't know —" She gave a sniff. "I didn't know anything had happened to him until yesterday." She choked down a sob. "It's still such a shock."

"I understand."

I really did. I'd gone through the same emotions myself.

Cocoa sauntered over and dropped his chicken at her feet. She stared at it, unblinking.

"What's going to happen to Cocoa now?" It was a distraught whisper.

"I've taken him in," I announced. Luke raised an eyebrow. I hadn't told him of my decision yet; I was still getting used to the idea myself.

A dog owner. That was something I'd never been before.

"That's good. I was worried about him. My boyfriend's allergic, so I couldn't have him."

I was pleased she'd at least considered it. That showed she cared.

"Suzanne, the detective investigating the murder might want to speak to you. We told him Henry had an assistant, but I'm sorry, we didn't realize you had the day off."

Her eyes widened. "You mean he might think I'm a suspect?"

"Oh, nothing like that," I was quick to assure her, even though it was exactly like that. "Just so they know where you were."

"You mean give them my alibi." She gulped and sniffed again.

I nodded, avoiding her gaze. "Yes."

She sat on the stool and cradled the hot chocolate Luke had put in front of her. I noticed her nails were painted bright cobalt blue.

A thought occurred to me. "Suzanne, do you have keys to the bakery?"

She shook her head. "Henry always opened up. He got there much earlier than me."

"To set up the shop?"

"No, to start baking. He started at five every morning, without fail. There were the day's orders to fulfill, and he always made two batches of his peanut butter twists. They were the last thing he baked before he opened, so they'd be fresh. Everybody loved those." Her eyes filled with tears, and she struggled to hold them back.

That explained the early morning walks. I stifled a yawn. Seriously, I was going to have to phase those out or at least push them back an hour or two. Cocoa would adjust.

"Oh, I forgot." She dug in her jacket pocket and came out with a set of keys. "I don't have the shop keys, but I do have a spare for his house."

"His house?" I stared at her. "Why do you have those?"

"Henry takes a fishing trip a couple times a year. I mean, he *took* a fishing trip a couple times a year. He used to ask me to go in and feed the goldfish when he was gone." The blood drained from her face. "Oh, shoot. The goldfish!"

"I can get it," I said, even though I didn't know the first thing about looking after fish. "It would be good to pick up some of Cocoa's things too." I tugged at the chicken in the dog's mouth. He hadn't put it down since we got to the shop. He gamely played tug-of-war with me but was not giving up that chicken.

"That would be great." She handed me a key.

I pocketed it. At least that was one problem solved.

I turned my thoughts back to the murder.

"When did you start work?" I asked.

"Around a quarter to nine. I usually get there fifteen minutes before opening to get the shop ready. I put napkins into dispensers, wipe down the surfaces, that sort of thing. I'm normally done by noon."

That tracked with when I'd seen her there on the odd occasion I'd collected my order for the day. "You don't work afternoons?"

"No, I'm at college then. I'm doing my PhD, so I spend my afternoons researching, mostly."

"Oh. What subject?"

"Botany." She absently patted Cocoa, and he rested his head against her leg. He was fond of her; I could tell by the way he seemed to trust her. She was familiar to him—a reminder of Henry.

"Was there anyone who had a beef with Henry?" Luke asked, leaning forward over the counter, dish towel in his hands. "One of his customers, or someone he knew?"

Suzanne looked shocked. "No, not that I know of. Do you think someone he knew killed him?"

"It seems that way," I cut in, wondering if we should even be talking about this. "I mean, it looks like he let the person into the kitchen, or he left the door unlocked and they snuck in."

Suzanne was shaking her head. "No, he wouldn't have. Henry was really careful about that. He told me off once for leaving it open."

Interesting.

"Do people come to the back door of the bakery in the morning? Delivery people, maybe?" I was looking for a reason, any reason, why that door might have been open.

"Deliveries do go around the back, but they always knock. Henry never leaves the door unlocked. He has expensive equipment in there that he didn't want stolen."

That made sense. I had no idea how much top-range mixers and other baking equipment cost, but I imagined it could get pretty pricey.

"So there's no way someone could have just walked in unless Henry let them in?" I summed up.

"I don't think so, no." She shrugged and bit her lip to stop it from trembling.

Luke stared at me across the counter. "In that case, Henry *must* have known his killer."

I felt my skin prickle. That meant we probably did too.

Chapter 11

A Surprise Intruder

Cocoa and I set off for Henry's house not long after Suzanne left. With Luke manning the store, and it being a quiet sort of Monday, I figured it was as good a time as any. The house wasn't far—just a short walk from the Square, down one of those tree-lined residential streets full of old Victorian homes, each in its own stage of wear or restoration.

I always liked this part of Maple Ridge. Someday, I imagined, it would be a truly beautiful neighborhood again. But right now, it was caught in that awkward in-between: scaffolding here, dumpsters there, the occasional whir of a power tool breaking the morning calm. The town was changing. Growing. Filling with new faces and fresh paint.

And while I could appreciate the charm of a well-loved painted lady, I couldn't help but feel a little wistful. I liked Maple Ridge exactly as it was—small, close-knit, dependable. I wasn't quite ready for change. Not after everything else that had shifted lately.

Henry's house came into view. It stood out among the grander homes, a more modest, modern build tucked between two larger properties. It sat a little further back from the road, shy almost, like it knew it didn't quite belong. I paused at the end of the walk, studying it with a more critical eye than I'd ever bothered to before. Beneath its clean lines, I could see hints of something older—maybe it started life as a carriage house or a stable. There was history in its bones, even if it didn't shout about it.

A white picket fence bordered the yard—an actual, honest-to-goodness picket fence—and that was all it took to set Cocoa's tail thumping. He pulled on the leash with sudden excitement, eager to be on familiar ground again.

"Alright, alright," I told him, laughing a little as I unlatched the gate.

I crouched to his level before letting him off the lead, putting on my serious face even though he was already vibrating with anticipation.

"Listen, mister. We're here for a reason, not just for fun. So no digging, no barking, and absolutely no chasing the neighborhood cat."

Cocoa gave me a solemn look, which I knew better than to trust, and licked my nose anyway.

The moment I unhooked his lead, Cocoa took off like a furry torpedo. I watched him zigzag across the yard, nose to the ground, tail a metronome of joy. He paused to sniff a bush, then marked his territory on what was clearly a favorite tree. His whole body was pure enthusiasm.

I smiled despite myself.

Henry could've just let him out like this, I thought. Quick and easy. But no, every morning, rain or shine, he walked Cocoa. It was their routine.

I let out a long breath and took the key from my coat pocket, walking slowly up the path to the porch. The house looked the same as the last time I saw it. Quiet, still, tucked neatly between two grander neighbors.

It felt strange being here alone. Strange, and a little intrusive. Henry and I shared laughter and gossip across the bakery counter, but entering his home... it felt like crossing a line.

Still, I wasn't here to snoop. I just wanted to grab some basics for Cocoa. His favorite food, maybe a chew toy or two. Something that smelled like home. And, of course, feed the poor goldfish, if it was still swimming.

How often do you feed a goldfish, anyway? I pulled out my phone and asked the question aloud, letting the voice assistant work its magic. I was halfway through the word "aquarium" when I noticed something odd.

The front door was ajar.

From the street, you'd never notice it, but from the porch, it was obvious. The door wasn't shut.

I froze. My mind offered up the most rational explanation first: maybe someone else came to feed the fish. A neighbor, a relative. Someone with a key and good intentions.

Please let it be that. Please let it just be someone feeding the fish.

My mouth went dry.

I hovered there on the porch, heart thudding, phone still in my hand. Should I call the police? Probably. But when I imagined explaining why I was inside a house that wasn't mine, I hesitated. I didn't have a legal right to be here, not really. And if it turned out to be a family member inside, what would I say? *Sorry, I just came to check on the dog and feed the fish?*

I sighed, unable to get rid of that sense of unease. I didn't feel like I belonged here.

But Cocoa clearly did.

This was still his home, and he had no hesitation. He trotted back to the front steps, tail wagging, and nudged the door wider with his nose like he'd done a hundred times before. Then, with a little bounce of his front paws, he disappeared inside.

"Cocoa!" I hissed, scrambling in after him.

The scene that greeted me stopped me in my tracks.

Chaos. Utter, unmistakable chaos.

Books and papers were flung across the floor like a hurricane had swept through. The television was unplugged and dragged halfway across the room. Pillowcases were stuffed with things and left slumped like sacks in the middle of the floor.

Then, from somewhere deeper in the house, I heard a loud crash. Furniture being overturned.

Cocoa stood stiffly in the center of the room, ears up, body taut. A low growl rumbled from his chest. His whole posture screamed "alert."

I didn't need a neon sign to understand what was happening.

I was in the middle of a burglary.

My fingers fumbled on the phone still clutched in my hand, but they were clammy, and it slipped and clattered to the floor. Before I could dive for it, Cocoa took off, barking furiously, claws scrambling on the hardwood.

"No! Cocoa, no—stop! Come here!" I whisper-yelled after him, panic flaring in my throat. "Cocoa! Bad dog! COCOA!"

He didn't even slow down.

And just like that, any hope of staying safe, staying rational, staying out of the line of fire was gone. My phone lay somewhere among the mess, unreachable. My heart pounded in my ears.

I did the only stupid thing I could think of. I went after him.

Most burglars don't want a fight, I reasoned. They just want to get in, grab what they can, and get out. They don't want to hurt anyone.

I hoped this one was like most burglars.

The hallway was long and wide, lined with open doors. I passed a bathroom on the left, a bedroom on the right. They were both empty. Cocoa's barking echoed from farther ahead, loud and frantic, but I couldn't tell which room it came from. There were two at the end of the hall. One left, one right.

Then I heard a shout, followed by a large—

BANG!

I dropped to the floor with a startled yelp, heart crashing into my ribs. But it wasn't a gun.

Another BANG!—something heavy being thrown, maybe a lamp or a bookend—and I realized they were aiming at my dog.

At Cocoa.

I didn't think.

I just scrambled up, legs shaking, and threw myself toward the noise, ready to defend my idiot dog with everything I had.

"No one throws anything at my dog!" I yelled.

And then I barreled in.

Chapter 12

It's Her Mess Now

Cocoa, as it turned out, didn't need saving.

He was leaping and barking with glee at a woman perched on top of a dresser across from the bed. Not attacking—just full of boundless enthusiasm, tail wagging like this was the best game he'd played in weeks.

The woman, meanwhile, was swearing like a sailor.

"What do you think you're doing?" I demanded, more baffled than angry.

She jolted at the sound of my voice and very nearly fell, which only encouraged Cocoa further. He pranced in place, clearly under the impression that she was tossing things for his entertainment.

Sometimes, I swear, that dog had more energy than sense.

The woman twisted to glare at me. Small in stature, but full of attitude. "What?"

"What. Are. You. Doing. Up. There?" I repeated, slower this time.

I really, really wished I'd called the sheriff.

She wasn't as young as I'd first assumed. Her mass of bleached curls gave a wild sort of impression, but her face had seen more than a few years. Lines bracketed her mouth, and her expression had a hardened, weather-worn set that only came from age. She shifted, trying to balance, and nearly slipped again.

Honestly, the top of the dresser wasn't built for perching —especially not for someone with... let's say, a generous sense of personal space.

"Can you at least grab the dratted dog?" she snapped.

She didn't say dratted, of course. But I mentally censored it for the sake of my sanity.

Cocoa, bless him, looked thrilled. His tongue lolled out the side of his mouth, eyes sparkling with delight. I reached for his collar anyway and held him in place while she clambered her way down.

I didn't offer to help.

"I have a right to be here," she declared, planting a foot on an open drawer like it was a rung on a ladder. "I was married to him. Half the stuff in this place is mine."

I blinked. Married? Henry?

That was news to me. Pretty major news, actually. The kind of detail you'd think might come up at some point, especially when arranging dog care.

She made her descent with more noise than grace and landed with a thud that made the floorboards tremble. Standing there, hands on hips, she squared off with me like I was the intruder. Which, fair enough, I was... but at least I wasn't ransacking the place.

I gestured toward the bed. "You want to explain all that?"

A pile of small electronics sat in the middle of the

comforter. Wireless speakers, smart home devices, even a fairly new tablet. I never took Henry for a gadget guy, but here we were.

She shrugged. "I told you. My stuff."

"When exactly were you married to him?" I asked. "Because Henry never mentioned a wife. And you clearly didn't know he had a dog."

She blinked at Cocoa. "He had a dog?"

Cocoa stared back at her, unimpressed.

"Okay, maybe it's been a few years," she admitted.

I pointed to one of the smart devices. "That version came out last year. I got one for Christmas. So unless you had a time machine..."

She didn't even blink. "Call it a replacement for the one I left behind."

"Pretty sure that's not how it works."

"It works just fine for me."

That was it. I let go of Cocoa's collar—figured she could deal with the consequences—and stalked back into the living room to find my phone and call the sheriff.

"What can I do for you, Miss Holloway?"

The sheriff's voice oozed that lazy charm some men cultivate when they've been in their job too long and haven't had a real emergency in months. He sounded more like someone manning a barbecue than someone leading a murder investigation. Which, honestly, fit with the general sense I'd had that he'd be happier sweeping this whole mess under the rug than actually solving it. I wondered where Detective Maddox was.

"Sheriff, it's Tess Holloway. I'm at Henry Dawson's house and there's a woman here tearing the place apart."

"You're at Henry Dawson's house?"

"Yes." I clenched the phone. "I stopped by to get some things for the dog. Did you hear what I just said? There's a woman here—"

"Yvonne's there?"

I blinked, pulled the phone away from my ear, and glanced at the woman in question.

"Are you Yvonne?"

"Yvonne Ortega. What's it to you?" she snapped, dragging a bundled comforter down the hallway like Santa Claus on a mission. It was obviously full of stuff, judging by the shape and weight. Cocoa was trailing behind, growling low, occasionally nipping at the fabric like it was a tug toy.

I brought the phone back to my ear. "Yes. Yvonne Ortega."

The sheriff sounded utterly unbothered. "Well, that's okay then."

"What do you mean that's okay? She's hauling half the house out to her car!"

"She's his ex-wife. Next of kin, technically. It's her mess now."

"That doesn't mean she can grab whatever she wants. There's got to be a process. A will. An executor—"

Behind me, Yvonne muttered, "Some people just don't understand grief."

She stuffed a wooden owl into the comforter like that proved a point.

"You're looting the place," I said, then raised my voice. "Sheriff, she's looting the place."

He sighed. "Let her take the knick-knacks. It's not worth the trouble trying to stop her."

"Sheriff, these aren't knick-knacks. These are Henry's belongings." I felt my blood pressure reach dangerous levels.

"If she has a key, I'm not going to stop her. Henry Dawson is deceased. She may as well take the stuff off our hands."

He just didn't want to deal with it. That much was obvious.

"Is Detective Maddox there?" I asked, fuming. "I'd like to speak to—"

And just like that, the line went dead.

Of course it did.

I turned in time to see Yvonne disappear out the door, the comforter still clutched in her arms. She was loading everything into a beat-up old Mercedes parked at the curb. It had one mismatched hubcap and an air of long-suffering neglect.

She made a few more trips. I stood there, too stunned and too mad to stop her. When she hoisted the TV up like it was the cherry on top of her haul, I considered hurling a squeaky toy at her head.

Instead, I retreated to the kitchen.

"Let's get your stuff, okay?" I told Cocoa, who at least looked like he was feeling mildly guilty about his lack of helpfulness.

I rooted around in the pantry until I found a few cans of food and jotted down the kibble brand from the bag tucked behind a mop. There was a tangle of toys in the corner, so I grabbed a few, shoving them into a plastic bag along with the cans. A ragged chew toy stuck out from under a pile of papers in the living room and I yanked it free, accidentally bringing a clump of unopened mail with it.

Yvonne breezed past one last time. "Be a doll and lock up when you leave."

The door slammed.

Cocoa sat and stared at it.

I stared at him. "You were a real asset to the team today, buddy."

He let out a sigh and dropped his head onto his paws.

I dropped the chewy bone into the bag, then hesitated with the mail still in my hands. It felt wrong to dig through someone else's letters, even if that someone was... no longer with us. But I couldn't bring myself to toss it back on the floor, so I walked it over to the desk and placed it down.

That's when I saw it.

A signature. One I recognized.

Peter Lane.

I frowned and picked the letter back up. My fingers itched with the guilt of reading it, but it wasn't a federal crime if the intended recipient was dead... right?

And besides. I thought I'd just found something important.

The letter was short. Polite. But clear.

Peter Lane was writing to ask Henry to reconsider his refusal to sell the bakery.

Chapter 13

Something Useful

I almost forgot the goldfish.

I was halfway down the front path, Cocoa tugging eagerly at the leash, before it hit me. The fish. The actual living creature Suzanne asked me to look after.

With a groan, I turned around and headed back inside, trying not to think about how many times today I'd walked in and out of this house like a revolving door of chaos.

Carrying the bowl back to the store was, in hindsight, a terrible idea. Especially with one overenthusiastic black Lab prancing ahead like this was some grand parade and not a delicate mission involving sloshing water and a very unimpressed goldfish.

I had the bowl tucked awkwardly under one arm, trying to keep it level, Cocoa's bed in a garbage bag in my hand, and the lead in the other. But every time Cocoa lunged toward a smell or a leaf or a bird, the water rose up like a tiny wave and splashed against my shirt.

By the time I made it back to the bookstore, there was maybe an inch of water left in the bowl. The fish was still alive. Just. Floating in the corner with a look I could only describe as judgmental.

I didn't blame it.

Cocoa followed me, tail wagging as if all was right in the world.

"What took you so long?" Luke asked, as I dropped the bag and *thunked* the goldfish bowl on the bar counter.

"That, and Henry's extremely annoying ex-wife."

His eyes widened. "Ex-wife?"

"Yeah. He's not even in the ground yet and she was ransacking the place. Can you believe it?"

He frowned. "Is that even allowed?"

I pulled Cocoa's old bed out and laid it in the corner of the bookstore, behind the till. He immediately went to lay in it. "I don't think so, but when I called the sheriff, he wasn't interested. Told me to let her have at it."

Luke shook his head, eyes on the goldfish. "That guy needs to retire—the sooner, the better."

"I'll second that." I nodded at the disgruntled goldfish. "What should we do about that?"

"I'll put some more water in the bowl and feed it, and it should be good to go."

"Go where?" I asked.

The bell jangled and Gina walked in carrying a sandwich. "Since you guys don't stock peanut butter twists anymore, I have to get my lunch elsewhere," she complained.

I groaned. "I'm working on getting another supplier. I just really don't want to go to Sophie." That seemed so wrong. Henry spent his last few years berating her for stealing his customers, and I didn't want to betray him by ordering from her now that he was dead.

Gina nodded. "I totally get it." She nodded at the goldfish. "You want that?"

"No," Luke and I said in unison.

She laughed. "I'll take it off your hands. My niece's birthday is coming up and I'm sure she'd like a goldfish."

Excellent. Another problem solved.

The day was looking up. I told her about Henry's ex stealing all his belongings. "I literally couldn't stop her, and Cocoa was no help."

In his bed, Cocoa gave an embarrassed whine.

"And so you should be," I admonished. Great, now I was having conversations with a dog.

"I see you two are getting along," Gina said, grinning. Luke, who'd been busy with the coffee machine, set a foaming latte down in front of her.

"Luke, I swear, you read my mind."

He smiled. "Just doing my job."

I glanced across at him. "Don't you have lectures today?"

"Yes, this afternoon. I'm going to head off in half an hour or so."

"With Lindy?"

"Yeah."

"Do you think you could ask her for an update on the fingerprints on the knife that was used to stab Henry?"

"I definitely will," he said with a nod. "There may have been other forensic evidence as well. I'll see what I can find out."

"Great. Oh, I meant to tell you: look what I found at Henry's place." I took out the letter signed by Peter Lane and spread it on the bar counter. Both Luke and Gina peered over to get a better look.

"Whoa!" Luke exclaimed. "This says that Peter wanted to buy the bakery."

"He is something of an amateur property developer," Gina said, frowning.

"I thought he was in the restaurant business." I shook my head as if to clear it. "I'm still trying to get a table at Flint + Flame."

"Don't waste your time." Luke pulled a face. "It's totally overpriced for what you get. Nobody wants a few morsels on their plate. That won't fill you up."

"How d'you know?" I asked, intrigued. "You manage to get a table?"

"I went once, when it first opened." I could have sworn Luke was blushing. "First date."

"I see. And what happened to this date?"

"Fizzled out after a few months." He shrugged. "Nothing new. I don't have the best luck with women."

I laughed. He was so young. "There's plenty of time," I told him.

Gina patted him on the back. "You're only twenty-one, Luke. You've got your whole life ahead of you to fall in love."

"Twenty-two, actually," he corrected.

She tilted her head, a smile tugging at her lips. "Noted."

"Let's get back to the letter," I said. "If Henry refused to sell, does that give Peter Lane a motive?"

"If that was his plan, it wasn't a very good one," Gina pointed out. "The property would go to probate, along with Henry's house and other assets, and then the court would decide what to do with them."

"With no heirs, they'd put them up for sale, surely?" I said. "Peter might get the place for a steal."

Gina was nodding. "It would take a long time though. These things move at a glacial pace."

I sighed. She was right. Although, maybe Peter was a patient man.

"I think I'll go and talk to him," I said.

They both looked at me in surprise.

I shrugged. "What? Just a friendly chat. I'll ask him why he wanted to buy the bakery."

"He'll ask how you knew about that," Luke pointed out.

"I'll say Henry told me. He doesn't need to know I found his letter."

Gina pursed her lips. "That's one way of getting an answer."

Luke finished cleaning the coffee machine and wiped his hands on the dish towel. "This is cool. We're like amateur sleuths, investigating Henry's murder."

"Well, the sheriff isn't doing anything to help," I muttered. Neither was that fancy Boston detective, by the looks of things. I hadn't seen or heard from him in days.

"I ran into that detective this morning," Gina said, as if reading my mind. "What was his name again?"

"Maddox," I supplied.

She glanced at me. "He's very good looking."

I shrugged. "If you like that kind of thing." He was big, brawny, and handsome, sure, but his personality left a lot to be desired. Grumpy didn't even begin to cover it.

She smiled. "He was at the bakery, poking around. I think I saw him go into Sophie's patisserie after that."

Now that was interesting.

"I wonder what Sophie was doing outside the bakery on the morning of Henry's murder," I mused.

Gina raised her eyebrows. "Why don't I ask her?"

I shook my head. "What? No. You don't have to do that."

She put her hands on her hips. "Why not? I want to. With you two sleuthing, I want to do my part too. Sophie's the obvious suspect, so it would be good if we could rule her out."

"Well, you can't just ask her outright for her alibi," I reasoned.

"Of course not, but we know each other pretty well. I'll find a more subtle way of getting it."

I broke into a smile. It was hard not to, given their enthusiasm. "Okay, then. Why not?" Maybe we could make some sense of all this. For Henry.

She clapped her hands together. "This is fun." Then she immediately sobered. "I mean, it's not fun that Henry's dead, but doing this with you guys is fun."

I had to agree. For the first time since that horrible morning, I felt like I was doing something useful.

Chapter 14

Detective Boston

I spent the rest of the day alone in the bookstore. Not alone, but with Cocoa. Although he slept for most of it. I was in the middle of recommending a dark romance novel to a sophomore literary student when the door jangled and in walked Detective Boston himself. He seemed to fill the doorway with his broad shoulders and six-foot-something frame, and I swear a shadow fell over the interior.

He nodded and stood in the entrance, hovering. Well, he'd just have to wait. I was busy with a customer. The student bought the first three in the series and left, so without any other excuses, I turned to Maddox.

"Good afternoon," I said, walking behind the bar as if it offered some sort of physical protection. His presence seemed to supersede that. "Can I get you a coffee?"

He eyed the shining cream-and-chrome contraption and came over. "Black would be good."

I could have guessed that would be his order. He didn't strike me as a cream-and-sugar kind of guy.

It didn't take long. I even made myself one, either to kill more time before the inevitable questions began or just because I knew I'd need it.

"So, what brings you here, Detective?" I asked, leaning on the bar counter. I couldn't bring myself to go and sit next to him on a stool. This wasn't a social visit, and he made me nervous. Not only did he remind me of the big city and the disaster of a life I left there, but he had that austere air about him that made me think he was someone who took life way too seriously. I guessed in his business, he had to.

"I heard you had a run-in with Henry Dawson's ex-wife this morning."

Bad news sure traveled fast. "Sheriff Grady tell you that?"

A nod. "I believe she was taking some of her things?"

"*His* things." The heat of indignation rose in my cheeks as I remembered her audacious behavior. "She was literally stealing his belongings, and right in front of me. The sheriff refused to do anything about it."

His gaze fixed on my face. "And what were you doing there?"

"I—I was there to pick up some of Cocoa's things. I thought if he had something familiar, he might not feel so displaced."

From his bed, Cocoa lifted his head and yawned.

"Oh, and I took the goldfish."

"Goldfish?" I saw him blink in surprise. He hadn't been expecting that answer.

"Yes, Henry's goldfish. Suzanne—that's his assistant—asked me to feed it, and I couldn't just leave it there, so I brought it back to the shop."

He glanced around. "Where is it?"

"My friend Gina took it for her niece." Why was he so interested in the darn goldfish?

He wasn't, as it turned out, for he steered the conversation back to Yvonne.

"Did you know Henry was married?" he asked.

"He wasn't. He was divorced, and I can see why."

The detective's eyes crinkled, just a little bit. Maybe he was human after all.

I sighed. "No, I didn't know about his ex, but then I've only been in town six months."

"Where were you before that?" he asked, but his tone suggested he already knew the answer.

"Boston."

He gave a quick nod. "Why'd you leave?"

I hesitated. How was this relevant? But he was waiting for an answer, his gaze still fixed on me over his coffee cup.

I cleared my throat. "Oh, you know. Stressful job, messy divorce, that kind of thing. I felt like I needed a change of scene."

"So you came out here?"

It wasn't that far away. "It's only three hours from Boston," I pointed out.

"Why here?" he asked, and I suddenly realized he wasn't here to talk about Henry's ex-wife—he wanted to talk about me. A lump formed in my throat. I thought Grady had cleared me as a suspect.

"No particular reason." Suddenly I didn't feel like talking anymore. As if sensing my tone, Cocoa came over and stood beside me. I patted his head, appreciating the silent moral support. He had my back, even if nobody else did.

Maddox's eyes narrowed. "You're telling me you just got in your car and drove out here, then decided to stay?"

I agreed, it sounded suspicious. Drawing in a deep breath, I said, "Actually, you're not far wrong. I was on my way to

Lake Morey for a vacation when I took a wrong turn and ended up in Maple Ridge. I thought it was a quaint little town, so I stayed for a few days. That's when I noticed the bookstore was for sale."

He spread his arm around, and I nodded.

"That's right. I was looking for a new... venture, so I put in an offer. It was a low offer, and I didn't expect to get it, but the owner was the son of the previous owner who'd passed away and just wanted to offload it as quick as possible. I got lucky."

"You bought it on a whim?" He stared at me, a flicker of disbelief in those fathomless dark eyes.

"Yes. Haven't you ever done anything spontaneous before?"

He didn't reply.

I shrugged—probably not. "It felt like the right decision. And it was. I renovated it and I'm very happy here."

"What was it you did in Boston?"

I couldn't prevent the shudder that followed that question. "I was editorial director for a publisher."

"Struik Books?"

I knew then that he knew exactly what I'd done and was just testing me.

"That's the one." I studied him for a long moment, but his chiseled features gave nothing away. He'd make a really good poker player. "Why are you asking me these questions, Detective, if you already know the answers?"

"I'm just doing my job, ma'am."

"Well, I have to do mine, so if there's anything else?" I put my hands on the bar counter and stood up.

"Did you know Henry Dawson before you came to town?" he asked.

I slid back down onto my stool. "What? No, of course not. The first time I met him was when I went next door to order pastries for my bookstore. As you can see, I haven't found a replacement yet."

"I believe there is another bakery in town."

I shook my head. "Oh, no. I wouldn't buy from Sophie. Henry wouldn't want it."

He gave me a strange look.

"What can I say? I'm a loyal friend."

His face softened, just a little bit, but enough to get rid of the hard edges that made him seem so severe. He was so much better looking when he wasn't frowning.

"So you didn't know anyone from Maple Ridge before you drove into town that day? When was it? Six months ago?"

"January, yes. And no, I didn't." I could tell he couldn't get his head around how someone could just take a wrong turn, fall in love with a place right away, and want to live here. Maple Ridge was that kind of town.

Now, here I was six months later—owner of a bookstore. I had friends, a community. And a dog.

"Why did you leave your job, Miss Holloway?"

I hesitated. What did that have to do with anything? "I was overworked and under-appreciated. I got passed over for promotion several times and decided to rethink my career choices."

Life choices.

He nodded. If he was hoping to find out I'd been fired, or left because of a scandal, he was going to be disappointed. I really was just unhappy.

"Is Holloway your maiden name or your married name?"

I stared at him. "My maiden name. I reverted to it after the divorce." Why did I get the feeling he already knew that too? "Detective, I really don't see—"

"Why did you file for divorce? It was you who filed, wasn't it?" Those eyes again, probing into my soul.

But my walls went up. I'd had enough. "My marriage status is not relevant to the case."

"It might be," he countered.

"My husband cheated on me, okay? Is that reason enough for you?" I was working long hours, always at the office. He got bored.

Maddox didn't respond.

"Am I a suspect, Detective?"

"I am trying to prove that you are not, Miss Holloway," he said, getting up off the stool. "You were the one to find Henry's body, you were alone on the street when he was murdered, and you have no alibi."

Was he kidding?

"Firstly, I wasn't out on the street when Henry was murdered. He'd been dead for at least twenty-five minutes when I found him, and at that point I was in the bookstore. I only went out because I saw Henry's dog."

Beside me, Cocoa gave a low growl. He didn't like the turn of conversation either.

"How do you know the time of death?" He scowled at me like I'd done something wrong. "We don't have the autopsy results back yet."

I shot him a look. "Because I took the peanut butter twists out of the oven. Henry must have put them in just before he was stabbed. They had started to burn, which means they must have been in for at least twenty-five minutes, half an hour at the most."

That would put the time of death at around eight o'clock, roughly speaking.

Maddox studied me, his dark eyes raking over my face, but I was on a roll, so I kept talking. "It was when I noticed Cocoa's bloody paws I decided to go and check on Henry."

"That's when you saw Sophie Beaumont."

"Yes, she was alone in the street. If you want a suspect, go and question her."

"I have, and she has an alibi for the time of Henry's murder."

"She does?" I was surprised. There hadn't been anyone with her when I'd seen her.

"She does," he said, tight-lipped as usual.

I raised my hands. "Well, the first time I saw him on Saturday morning was when I found his body." A lump formed in my throat, and I reached for my coffee.

Thankfully, a gaggle of teenage girls walked in, talking and giggling loudly. I set my cup down on the counter. "Are we done here?"

He glanced at the girls, then nodded. "Yes, Miss Holloway. I believe we are."

I turned my back on him to serve the teenagers and didn't look around until I heard the bell jingle as he walked out. There he was, stalking off down the street, the scowl firmly back on his face.

It was only then I realized I'd forgotten to tell him about Peter Lane.

Chapter 15

BLT With Avocado

The restaurant was a lot bigger than I expected, at least three times the size of my little bookstore. What made it really charming, though, was the outdoor seating. It was tucked into a narrow alley between the restaurant and the building next door, but somehow it didn't feel cramped. There was a big stone fireplace anchoring the space, and I could just imagine how cozy it must be in winter, with the flames flickering and people huddled under blankets, sipping hot drinks.

Today, though, it was all bright sunshine and cheerful chatter, with sleek gray umbrellas shading the tables like little islands of calm.

The food looked good, and my stomach rumbled. I remembered I'd skipped lunch amid the fiasco at Henry's. Cocoa licked his lips next to me, clearly in agreement. I wondered if they allowed dogs.

My question was answered a few moments later, when a coiffed hostess in head-to-toe black came forward. "I'm afraid no pets allowed," she told me.

Dilemma. I could see there were still tables available, and Peter Lane was inside, walking around charming guests.

"Okay, give me ten minutes," I said, and walked off in the direction of the optician.

Luckily, Gina was just closing up. She looked tired, like she wanted to get home and relax, and I felt bad thrusting Cocoa on her.

"It's just for an hour," I promised, ignoring the way Cocoa was looking at me. "Then I'll swing by and pick him up."

She took the leash. "That's okay, don't worry. I'll give him something to eat. I've got to feed Iris anyway."

Then I remembered Gina had a dog too, a lovely border collie. I'd met them out walking once. Iris was at home with her husband, a physics professor. They lived on campus, so he was home a lot.

I thanked her and headed back to the restaurant.

I could hear my wallet screaming in protest as I walked in the door. "Table for one," I told the hostess.

Within minutes I was seated at a table by the window staring at a menu with the kinds of prices that make your eyes water. It was my only meal of the day, I rationalized. Not too bad if you think of it that way.

Still, I winced as I ordered a BLT with avocado and a glass of tap water. Luke was right—this place was horribly overpriced.

On the bright side, it was a truly beautiful evening. The sun was setting at the end of Main Street, casting the entire town in a rosy golden glow. Only the garish yellow tape across the front door of the bakery spoiled the view.

I watched Peter Lane as he strode between tables, smiling and bowing to his customers, pausing to talk to his more important guests. He had the smooth good looks of a man used to money. His tan was fake, probably sprayed on, and his smile was almost too suave. His expensive suit was a good cut, but he didn't have the type of frame Detective Boston had. He didn't fill the suit like Maddox did.

I frowned, wondering where that thought had come from. It was likely just because he'd been growling at me in my bookstore for the last hour.

Peter Lane walked past my table. I could tell he wasn't going to stop, since I was a woman alone and nobody of importance. So I stood up.

He glanced my way, his eye drawn by my movement. "Mr. Lane." I held out my hand. "It's good to see you again."

He nodded. "Miss Holloway. My apologies, I didn't see you there."

Liar. He knew exactly who I was—he just had bigger fish to fry. Excuse the pun.

"That's alright. This is my first time here. I thought I'd give it a try."

"That's awesome. I'm sure you'll enjoy your meal." His confidence was staggering.

"Mr. Lane, do you mind if I ask you a question? It's about Henry."

He frowned. "Please, call me Peter. No, I don't mind. Henry was a friend."

Another lie?

"I was just wondering what happens to the bakery now that Henry's... gone."

He shook his head, confused. "I'm not following."

"I mean, I know you wanted to buy it. I was just wondering if you were still interested in doing so."

There was a long pause, and I could see the cogs turning in Peter's brain. "How did you know I wanted to buy the bakery?" he eventually asked, his full attention on me now.

I smiled. "Henry told me."

"Oh, I see. I didn't realize—" He stopped, bit his lip, then said, "It doesn't matter. Henry left the bakery to a third party, in his will."

"His will?"

There was a will? Nobody had even mentioned a will.

"That's what his lawyer told me."

"So you did inquire?"

He shrugged. "Thought it was worth asking. Even if there wasn't a will, the property would be tied up in probate for months, maybe even years."

"I understand." My theory that the bakery gave Peter a motive to kill Henry just flew out the window.

"What's it to you, anyway?" he asked, studying me. "Did you want to put in an offer?"

"I was thinking about it." Now I was lying, but I couldn't think of another excuse for my questioning. "It doesn't matter now, though. It was just an idea."

He nodded. "I'd better go. Enjoy your meal, Miss Holloway."

He moved on, and I was left ruminating on what he'd said. Henry had left the bakery to a mysterious third party. That was intriguing. There was a piece on this chessboard that we didn't know about yet.

I was going to make it my business to find out who that was.

Chapter 16

Playing It Cool

Cocoa

I was in love. It was official.

Iris was... incredible. That soft black-and-white fur. Those keen, intelligent eyes, framed by little freckles around her snout. The way her ears tilted with precision, like she was listening for a secret. And I loved that long, silky tail, with just the right amount of wave. She held it high in a show of natural confidence.

She was elegant. Regal, even. A proper lady. No drooly jowls, no unseemly butt-sniffing. She didn't bark at garden gnomes or chase her own tail. She glided, her herding prowess obvious in every movement.

I was, in short, a mess.

I had tried to impress her earlier with a nice roll in the flower bed. You know, show her my wild side. My earthy, grounded personality. She wasn't looking. I tried again with a playful bark and a high-speed lap around the birdbath, but she barely glanced up. She was unmoved by raw athleticism. I respected that.

Her human was just like her. Small and graceful, with soft copper curls and long lashes. If she were a dog, she'd be a Cavalier King Charles spaniel—fancy but not fussy. The kind of person who smelled like lavender and roast chicken, which was... honestly, a pretty winning combo.

Anyway, Tess left me there while she went off to meet someone. I'm not sure who. She told me to be on my best behavior. I was. Mostly. Except for the flower bed incident.

The garden was quiet now, warm sun dappling through the slats of a wooden fence. I lay down in the grass, careful to angle myself so I was facing Iris. Just in case she decided to notice me. She was lying under a rose bush, paws crossed like she owned the place.

I sighed dramatically.

That was when the gate creaked open.

I sat up, alert and in guard mode, but it was just another human. A familiar one. I knew her scent—caramel, butter, and a whisper of flour.

She waved at Gina, and they exchanged greetings, their voices floating over the breeze. I trotted closer, pretending I was casually inspecting a stick. But I kept one ear tilted their way.

This was the woman who'd held on to me in the street outside Henry's on that terrible day. I recognized her voice.

"It's a good thing you were there to take care of Cocoa on Saturday morning," Iris's human was saying, pouring them each a glass of wine. White, not red. I knew because red smelled sharper and gave me the sneezes.

"He was out of control," the visitor said in her soft French accent. "I couldn't keep hold of him. He got away and ran straight back to that awful murder scene."

It's true. I had. Henry was there.

"The poor dog was traumatized," Iris's human said. "But I meant to ask, what were you doing on Main Street that early, anyway? I thought you'd be opening the patisserie."

Her tone was light, like she was asking about the weather. But there was something underneath it. A flicker of interest. A scent of... accusation? I tilted my head.

The visitor answered smoothly. "I was in the shop, baking. Like always. I got in around five."

"Same as Henry used to," Iris's human replied with a knowing nod.

There was a pause.

"Unlike Henry, though," the visitor added, "I don't work alone. My assistant, Noah, was with me."

Noah. I filed that away in the back of my brain. It's a good name. Short. Easy to bark.

"I popped out for ten minutes," the visitor continued. "Ran to Blooms to pick up some flowers for the store. It always cheers up the display."

Iris's human hummed thoughtfully. "You always pick the nicest bunches."

"I know. It makes the place so much brighter."

They kept talking, their voices drifting to other things— muffin recipes, something about a canceled order. I stopped listening.

I stretched out, gave a long yawn, then rolled onto my back with a grunt. The sun was toasty on my belly fur. Iris hadn't moved. She was still under the rose bush, cool and collected, watching a butterfly with great interest. Probably thinking deep, beautiful thoughts.

I flipped upright and did a full-body shake. Time to try again.

I grabbed a nearby squeaky toy from Gina's herb bed and pranced over to Iris. I would have offered her my chicken, but

I'd left it inside by the front door—forgotten the moment I laid eyes on her.

I dropped it near her paws. Not too close. I didn't want to seem desperate.

She didn't move.

I nudged it forward with my nose. Gave it a squeak. Subtle. Understated. Just enough to say, *Hey, I'm emotionally available and also squeaky.*

Finally, finally, she turned her head. Those eyes met mine. Assessing. Cool.

Then, to my utter delight, she rose and sauntered over.

Sniffed the toy.

Sniffed me.

I forgot how to stand properly for a second. My back leg twitched.

Then, glory of glories, she picked up my offering and trotted away with it.

A game.

It's a game!

I bounced after her, tail wagging so hard it nearly propelled me into a shrub. She paused near the garden bench and gave me a look over her shoulder that said, *Well, are you coming or not?*

Hell, yeah.

You didn't have to ask this mutt twice.

We played a little. Not rough—she's too refined for that. It was more like flirtation in motion. I pretended to sneak up, she pretended not to see. I darted forward, she leaped sideways with perfect grace. It was poetry. I think I was whining a little inside.

Eventually, we collapsed together under the shade of the climbing roses, panting lightly. Our paws almost touched.

I could hear the humans laughing again, their wine glasses

clinking. Whatever they were talking about, I was no longer interested. My job, right now, was simpler.

Make Iris love me.

Or at the very least, tolerate me long enough to share her water bowl. Which, for a first date, I'd say was pretty promising.

Chapter 17

What Third Party?

"We need to talk," I told Gina the moment I walked in. The sun had set, and dusk was falling over the town. "I have news."

"So do I," she said, just as her husband came into the kitchen. His office-slash-laboratory was out in the garden, away from the house.

"Just in case he blows anything up," Gina had told me the first time I'd been here.

"Oh, I didn't know we still had company," he said cheerfully. "Hello, Tess. How's the bookstore?"

"Going well, thank you, Phil," I replied, offering a smile. "Although we're all a bit upset by Henry's death."

"I heard about that. Poor guy. Henry was one of the good ones."

"He was, wasn't he?"

Gina tapped her nails on the table. "I wonder if Luke managed to speak to Lindy. Maybe he should be here too."

"I'll message him." I pulled out my phone and fired off a text.

His response was almost immediate. *Be right there.* It helped that Gina and Phil lived on campus, right next to the science building.

"How's Cocoa?" I asked, looking around. Neither he nor Iris were anywhere to be found.

"They're still in the garden," Gina said, smiling. "They totally hit it off. It might be true love."

"Really?" I laughed. A romance would help him get over the void Henry had left.

We took a seat at the square kitchen table while Phil hovered by the fridge. "Supper is going to have to wait, I'm afraid," Gina told him. "We've got a mystery to solve."

He came over. "What mystery?"

"Henry's murder, of course."

He stared at his wife. "Isn't that the sheriff's job?"

"Have you met the sheriff?" I asked.

He scoffed. "I guess you have a point."

"We're just looking into it casually," I said, not wanting Phil to worry unduly. "If we discover anything, we'll go directly to Detective Maddox."

"He the one up from Boston?" Phil asked.

"Yes, have you spoken to him?" Gina glanced up at her husband.

"No, but everyone's talking about him on campus. Seems he's made quite an impression on the young ladies at the college."

Gina shot me a knowing glance.

Thankfully, there was a knock on the door. "That will be Luke," I said.

"I'll get it." Phil went to let him in.

Luke came in, panting a little from the fast walk across campus.

"You okay?" I asked, noticing the lines on his usually smooth forehead. Something was bothering him.

"Yeah, I'm fine. It's just—I can't find my friend, Monty. I thought he was at his girlfriend's, but I bumped into her today and she hasn't seen him since Saturday morning."

"That's three days," Gina said.

I frowned. "Does he usually disappear like this?"

"No, that's the thing. Monty's working on his thesis—has been since last year. There's no way he'd take off for three whole days."

"Could he be on a research trip?" I guessed. It was possible, if he was working on a thesis.

"Maybe, but then why isn't he answering his cell?"

I didn't have the answer.

"Maybe he's gone home for the weekend," Gina suggested. "Have you tried his folks?"

"He lives in California. I don't think he'd drive there for the weekend, and if he booked a flight, I'd know about it."

"Maybe call them to check," Phil said, grabbing a beer out of the refrigerator.

"Yeah, I will." Luke sat down at the table. "But I did manage to speak to Lindy Huang today, and what she told me was very interesting."

"Oh yeah?" Both Gina and I leaned forward.

"Yeah. Apparently, the knife was clean. Not a fingerprint in sight."

"How can that be?" Gina asked. "Henry must have used that knife all the time."

"Unless the killer wiped it down."

I met Luke's gaze.

"Or it wasn't Henry's knife," he whispered.

I leaned forward. "The killer brought the knife with them

and wore gloves. That's why there are no prints on the weapon. It means this was a planned, premeditated murder."

"They're the same thing," Luke pointed out unhelpfully. "Planned and premedit—" He saw my look and shrugged. "Never mind."

"Well, at least that rules you out." Gina raised her eyebrows at me.

True. I hadn't considered that. Detective Boston could eat his words.

"It rules out Sophie too," I said, as an afterthought.

"That tracks with what she told me earlier this evening," Gina said.

I glanced up. "She was here?"

"Yes, she came over for a glass of wine. I had to buy a box of *chausson aux pommes* to get her here, but Phil won't complain."

"*Chausson* what?" Luke asked.

"It's just a French term for a folded apple pastry," I explained.

At his surprised look, I said, "I have an encyclopedic knowledge of all things sweet and gooey."

Gina laughed. "I knew there was a reason why we were friends."

"What did she say?" I asked, bringing the conversation back on track.

"Well, she gets to her bakery at five in the morning too, but she has a kitchen assistant who helps her—Noah. He can vouch for her, apparently."

"But she wasn't there—she was in the street outside Henry's bakery," I corrected. "At half past eight. I saw her myself."

"According to Sophie, she was on her way to buy some flowers from Blooms—for her counter display."

I knew from personal experience that Blooms opened at

eight, because I'd done the same thing before for the bookstore. Had she been carrying flowers when I'd thrown Cocoa at her? I couldn't remember. I'd been preoccupied at the time.

"Blooms must have confirmed. Detective Maddox said she'd been cleared from the investigation."

"Detective Maddox?" Gina looked quizzically at me. "When did you see him?"

"This afternoon. He stopped by while Luke was at lectures and asked me all kinds of questions—like why I was here in Maple Ridge and what I'd done back in Boston."

I didn't mention he'd also asked me about my divorce. It still stung having to admit that to a total stranger. I didn't want to revisit it again.

"He was looking into your background?" Gina asked, alarmed.

"Yes. He said he was trying to clear me as a suspect, but I think he was just digging."

"Well, you're in the clear now," Luke said, wiggling his fingers in the air. "No prints."

I exhaled. Yes, that was a relief.

Then I remembered what Peter had told me. "Oh, I almost forgot. I went to Flint + Flame this evening and spoke with Peter Lane. He told me something very interesting."

"What was it?" Luke asked. Gina gazed at me expectantly.

"Get this—Henry has left the bakery to a third party in his will."

"What?" they both cried in unison.

Luke recovered first. "What third party?"

I nodded across at him. "That, my dear Watson, is what we have to find out."

Chapter 18

Trespassers and Tattoos

I opened the bookstore just before nine, the bell above the door jangling as I stepped inside with Cocoa trotting faithfully at my side. The air inside was still cool from the overnight chill, carrying the familiar scents of paper, coffee grounds, and lemon-scented floor polish. I flicked on the lights, turned on the coffee machine, and took a moment to soak it all in.

There's something deeply comforting about a space filled with books. Their quiet presence. Their weight. The stories held gently between covers, waiting for someone to care enough to pick them up and read.

I was rearranging a stack of gardening books by the window when the door opened with its usual soft chime. I looked up and smiled.

"Carly. This is a nice surprise." Her jeans had paint

smudges on them, and there was a paintbrush sticking out of her hair, tied up in a messy bun.

"I've been working," she explained, waving a hand over her paint-splattered attire. "But I just popped out for a coffee and to see if you have any more books in that new series you recommended. I've read the first one already."

"The White Knight Trilogy? Yes, I've got the other two in stock."

As I went to get them, a thought struck me. Carly and her husband Bert were Maple Ridge locals. Maybe they could help us figure out who Henry's attorney was.

"Carly," I said, returning to the counter, "you've lived here for a long time, haven't you?"

"All my life," she said proudly. "I mean, I did a little stint in New York after art school—it's a rite of passage, isn't it?— but I came back afterwards. That's when I met Bert."

"Okay, because I'm wondering who Henry's lawyer was. Can you help?"

"His lawyer? Is something wrong, Tess?"

"Oh, no. Nothing like that. It's just—Henry apparently left the bakery to a third party, and nobody seems to know who it is. I was hoping he'd tell me."

"A third party," she mused. "How mysterious."

It was. I wished it were less so.

"Henry's lawyer?" I prompted.

She pulled out the paintbrush, scratched her head with it, then stuck it back into her bun. "Hmm... if I remember correctly, it's Simon Hsu."

"Thanks." I wrote it down on a till slip.

"But he's unlikely to tell you anything," Carly warned. "Attorney–client privilege and all that."

"But Henry's dead," I said.

"Even so. If the will hasn't been read, then he's not at

liberty to say anything—particularly to a stranger. No offense."

I wasn't a stranger. I was Henry's friend. But I got it. What she said made sense. I should have considered that.

My shoulders slumped. "Now what?"

She paused for a moment, then said, "Why don't you let me talk to him?"

I stared at her. "You know him?"

"Nope."

"Then why would he talk to you and not to me?"

She gave a secretive smile. "Because his daughter, Lily, is in my art class."

I was trying to walk a dog in love.

There's just no other way to describe it. Cocoa was smitten. Enamored. Completely and utterly besotted with Gina's elegant border collie, Iris. He was also still carrying that ridiculous stuffed chicken around like it was a badge of honor—or maybe an emotional support poultry. Honestly, I'd stopped trying to make sense of it.

"This isn't something I intend to make a habit out of," I said, as we ambled down Maple Ridge's main drag. "I mean, okay for now, but just so you know..."

Gina let out a warm laugh beside me. "Give him a break. He's been through a lot in the last few days. If he gets a little comfort from a chicken, is that so bad?"

I eyed the slobbery, slowly deteriorating plush toy and sighed. I was absolutely going to end up carrying that thing by the wing before this walk was over. Still, if it made Cocoa happy, I wasn't about to take that away from him.

In the meantime, he was doing that thing where he was trying to sniff the other dog, do a play bow, and wag his back end until it looked like his spine was about to detach.

Iris, for her part, stood perfectly still. Her plume of a tail gave a single dignified wave. Her dark eyes were serious, studious, as though she were evaluating Cocoa for some kind of mysterious canine scholarship.

Then—be still my heart—she bowed. Just a little, but it was enough. She mock-pounced, and Cocoa nearly dropped his chicken in surprise.

"Oh no you don't," I whispered, tightening my grip on the leash. "We were walking, remember?"

Carly smiled. "They're adorable."

The three of us had decided to touch base after work and take the dogs for a stroll. Unfortunately, Luke couldn't make it, since he had a midterm tomorrow and needed to study. Worryingly, his friend Monty still hadn't turned up, so I'd advised him to file a missing-person report at the sheriff's office.

Cocoa had thankfully gotten over his ludicrous 4 a.m. routine, as long as I let him out into the garden to pee. I had to make up for it, though, after work.

"So, what did Simon Hsu say?" I asked Carly. She'd been bursting to tell us ever since we set out.

She took a deep breath. "Well, there is a will—Peter Lane was right—but Simon doesn't know what's in it."

"What?" I stared at her.

"Didn't he draw it up?" Gina asked.

"No, he didn't. Henry was very secretive, apparently. He didn't want anyone to know who he'd left things to, so he wrote the will in private. Simon doesn't even know who witnessed it, although Henry assured him it was all legal."

"He has the will, though, right?" I asked. "I mean, why doesn't he just look?"

"That's the thing," Carly mused. "He doesn't have it. Henry kept it. He said when the time came, he'd hand it over."

"Except he didn't expect to die so soon," Gina whispered.

We all contemplated this.

"So, now what?" I asked as we turned a corner. "If the lawyer hasn't seen the will, how does he know there's a mysterious third party?"

Carly shrugged. "Henry must have bequeathed his estate to somebody."

A whine made me look down. The dogs had been trotting along side by side, tails high, ears perked, when suddenly, Cocoa stopped.

We were across from the bakery.

His tail wagged once, then stopped. The chicken slipped in his mouth, and his ears flattened.

Gina made a small, sympathetic noise. "Oh, that's sad."

"And that's concerning," I murmured, squinting toward the building. Someone was loitering near the alleyway, trying to peek in the windows. The police tape fluttered faintly in the breeze.

I took in the ripped jeans, white trainers, and salmon-colored shirt. "I think he might be from the media."

Carly's mouth tightened. "That's gruesome. Vultures."

"Hold him a sec." I passed the leash to Gina and strode across the street.

"Excuse me?" I called, voice firmer than I felt.

The man startled, his hand slipping from the edge of the glass as he turned around. For one ridiculous second, I thought he might run.

He didn't. But he did look mortified.

"Oh, sorry." He held his hands up, palms out, like I was about to frisk him. "Didn't mean to be weird. I just..."

He glanced at the tape. His eyes were wide behind chunky, tortoiseshell glasses, and up close I could see he wasn't nearly as rough as I'd assumed.

"You're standing in a taped-off crime scene," I said, channeling my mother's schoolteacher voice. "That area is off-limits."

He winced. "I know, but I wanted to see where Henry... how Henry died."

I frowned. "You knew Henry?"

A sad nod. "He and I go way back."

I swept a hair out of my face. "I'm sorry, and you are?"

He rubbed the back of his neck, revealing a series of tattoos on his arms—stars, a half-moon, and what looked unmistakably like a tiny wire whisk. A whisk? I blinked.

"My name's Buck Roberts," he said. "Henry was my mentor. He taught me everything I know."

I was momentarily dumbstruck. A million questions flew through my mind.

"You don't look like a Buck," I said, unable to stop myself.

He threw his head back and laughed, the sound high and musical, like a kettle whistling at a very fabulous tea party.

"I know! Everyone says that. I think my father was hoping for a rugged cowboy type, but instead—" he fluttered his fingers dramatically—"he got me."

He spread his arms in a joyful shrug, as if to say, *Ta-da, here I am!*

I liked him.

The others came over, Gina dragging both dogs with her. Cocoa was so focused on Iris that he barely even looked at the stranger. A lot of good he was as a guard dog.

"This is Buck," I told them. "He's a friend of Henry's."

"I only just got here," he explained. "I'm from New York."

"You're staying in town?" Gina asked.

"Yes, I came hoping to see Henry, but..." He shrugged.

Carly frowned. "You didn't know he was dead?"

"Not until I got here. The manager at the B and B told me. Is it true he was—" he dropped his voice to a conspiratorial whisper—"murdered?"

"It's absolutely true," I said. "How do you know Henry, again? I know you said he trained you, but—"

"I used to work here, at the bakery," he said. "It was a long time ago now. Nearly fifteen years. Hard to believe."

Carly blinked several times. "You're that Buck?"

He grinned. "In all my glory."

"You've changed so much I hardly recognized you."

"I know." He turned back to me and blew out his cheeks. "I was a fat kid, you see. I know we're not supposed to say that nowadays, but hey, there you have it. I still am, at heart. I've just learned some self-control over the years. Had to, in my profession."

"And what is that?" I asked.

"I'm a baker, like Henry." His smile slipped. "Although I'm just a lowly helper. I don't own my own bakery. Yet."

I glanced at the others. Was Buck the mysterious third party?

The dogs were getting boisterous again and tugging at the leashes in Gina's hand. She passed me Cocoa's leash back. We had to move on or risk them creating a scene.

I gave a hasty nod. "I've got to go, but I own the Book Mark bookstore and coffee bar next door. Why don't you stop in tomorrow and we can talk some more."

He grinned. "I'd like that."

I barely managed a wave as Cocoa took off after Iris, dragging me with him. Once I'd caught up to the others, I said, "That was interesting. What do we think of Buck?"

"I remember him as a kid," Carly said, frowning. "But he didn't look anything like he does now. If he hadn't said he used to work at the bakery, I'd never have guessed it was the same person."

"Strange, him appearing in town now," Gina said thoughtfully. "I mean, why come now, after all these years?"

I shook my head. All we had was questions, but I hoped that when Buck came round tomorrow, we'd find out some of the answers.

Chapter 19

Missing Monty

"I'm really worried," Luke admitted when he came into the bookstore the next morning. "Monty's parents don't know where he is either."

"He's still not back?" I frowned. "What did the sheriff say?"

"To contact campus security, which I did. They're out searching for him, but so far, nothing." He shrugged. "I've been to his room, but there's nothing to indicate where he might have gone."

"You've tried calling him again?"

"Of course. Repeatedly. His phone goes straight to voicemail."

I had to admit, this didn't sound good.

I took Luke over to the study table and we sat down. "Okay, let's conduct our own search. Where was he last seen?"

"At a frat party on Friday night. Everybody stayed over,

but he and Evie had one of their arguments, so he left. That was in the early hours. I assumed he'd gone back to the dorm, but he never arrived."

"Where was this frat party?" I asked.

"About a mile out of town, on the south side of the lake."

I got up and rummaged around the shelves behind me for a fold-up map of the area. We had several under the Travel section. Once I'd found what I was looking for, I spread it out over the table.

"Okay, show me the route he would have taken home that morning."

Luke scanned the map and put his finger on the location of the frat house. "He'd have walked from here, down to the lake, around it, and back up here to Main Street. Then he'd have walked down Acorn Avenue to the dorm."

I studied the route Luke had specified. "He wouldn't have gone along the street?"

He shook his head. "That's farther. The lake path is the shortcut. Everybody in that frat uses it to get to classes."

I looked at Luke. "How drunk was he when he left the party?"

The color drained from his face. "You think he stumbled and fell into the lake?"

"I'm saying it's a possibility we have to consider."

Luke dropped his head into his hands. "No. I can't even go there."

"Had he been drinking?" I asked.

"Yeah, but not much. Like I said, he was working on his thesis. I had midterms coming up, so neither of us were going for it."

"What time did he leave?"

Luke thought for a moment. "It must have been around four in the morning."

I blinked. "Some party."

He shrugged. "Not really. We just sat around talking and listening to music most of the night. Then most people crashed on the couches until morning."

I nodded, remembering my own college days.

"What about you?"

"I fell asleep. Left around seven the next morning. I wanted to get home and shower before I came into the bookstore."

"You walk the same way?"

"No, I had my bike. Didn't use the lake path."

I looked down at Cocoa, dozing on his bed. I couldn't leave the bookstore but... "Why don't you take Cocoa and walk to the frat and back, now that it's daylight."

I still prayed they'd find Monty safe and sound, but after four days, it wasn't looking likely. I didn't want to think he'd fallen into the lake, but like I'd told Luke, it was a very real worry. Campus security must be thinking the same thing.

He got up wearily. "I guess. I don't know what else to do."

"Have they tried tracing his phone?" I asked. "They might be able to pinpoint where he was when the battery died or it was switched off."

He shrugged. "You'd think so, but I don't know."

A bad feeling gnawed at my gut. The sheriff should have acted sooner. Campus security should have searched days ago.

"I'll call Detective Maddox," I decided. "Maybe he can shake things up a bit."

Relief flashed across his face. "If you could, Tess, that would be great."

"In the meantime, you and Cocoa try to retrace his steps."

Cocoa grunted from his bed and opened one eye.

Luke fetched the leash from behind the checkout desk and jingled it. "Walkies, Cocoa."

Cocoa leaped from sleeping to enthusiastic tail-wagging in one swift movement. It was admirable.

"See you later," I called after them as they disappeared out the door.

Detective Maddox arrived within half an hour. I felt his presence before he'd even stepped inside. "Morning, Miss Holloway. I came as soon as I got your message."

I'd called the sheriff's office and told them I needed to speak to him, knowing he'd think it was to do with the case. I did have some information to bargain with, but first I needed his help finding Monty.

"I'm glad you're here," I began, once he'd joined me at the study table. I had the map laid out in front of me and had marked the location of the frat house and the dorm.

"What's this?" His eyes flickered over the map.

I took a deep breath, then let the words out all in a rush. "I was hoping you'd be able to help us find a missing student."

His gaze narrowed. "What does this have to do with Henry Dawson's murder?"

"Er, nothing. At least I don't think it has anything to do with it."

Could it have? The thought hadn't occurred to me.

Before I could dwell on that, he said, "That's a matter for campus security."

"We've already called them," I said tersely—a combination of worry and too much caffeine. "But the kid is still missing and neither his best friend nor his parents know where he is. It's been four days."

The detective opened his mouth to say something, but I cut him off. "He was last seen in the early hours of Saturday morning, at a frat party on the other side of the lake. He walked home alone along the lake path. You need to get the police up here to start searching in the woods surrounding the lake." I paused. "And in the water."

"You think something bad has happened to him?" His dark eyes probed mine.

I gave a reluctant nod. "I hope it hasn't, but four days is a long time. They should have flagged him as a missing person days ago. Twenty-four hours, isn't it? That's how long before you can report someone missing?"

He gave a stiff nod. "That is the general rule, yeah."

I leaned so far forward I could smell his aftershave. "Detective, please help us find this missing kid. Or at least ask campus security for an update. Nobody knows what's going on, and I'm scared it may already be too late."

He paused for a beat, then took out his phone. "What's the boy's name?"

I breathed a sigh of relief, then gave him all the details I had, including Monty's dorm number and the address of the frat house. I showed him the route on the map. "Luke and Cocoa are there now, searching."

He got up. "I'll call campus security right away. I agree, something should have been done sooner."

"Thank you." I followed to see him out. "Oh, and I really do have some information about Henry's murder. It wasn't just a ruse to get you over here."

He stopped in his tracks. "You do?"

"Yes, but first make your call—that's much more important. Then we'll talk."

Detective Maddox gave me a long, intense look, then stalked out, phone in hand.

Henry was already dead. He wouldn't mind if we concentrated on this first. In fact, if I knew Henry, he'd insist on it.

Chapter 20

A Full Sweep

The sun had already begun its lazy descent by the time I made it down to the lake. Detective Maddox hadn't come back to find out what it was I knew about Henry's case. Something else must have come up, and then the search operation got underway.

Long shadows stretched across the path, adding an ominous touch. The air held that late-summer stillness, where even the breeze seemed reluctant to stir.

The lake was buzzing. Not with joy or summer frivolity, but with tension. Students, faculty members, campus security —half the college, it seemed—had come out to help in the search.

Small clusters combed the edge of the woods, methodically spaced apart, eyes on the ground. The sound of walkie-talkies crackled here and there. Even the birds seemed to have quieted, as if they knew what was at stake.

I spotted Luke and Cocoa near the water's edge. Luke's tall frame was easy to pinpoint, silhouetted against the glimmer of the lake. He held Cocoa's leash in one hand and was scanning the waterline, as if willing Monty to appear from the depths. I approached slowly, not wanting to break his focus.

"Hey," I said gently.

Cocoa came over and butted my leg with his head. I gave him a quick ear scratch.

Luke turned, eyes rimmed red. "They've been diving for over an hour and haven't found a thing."

I reached out and placed a hand on his shoulder, though my throat tightened. "I'm sorry, Luke."

He shook his head. "I should've walked back with him. If I had, he might not be missing."

"You can't think like that. This isn't your fault." I meant it, but guilt doesn't always listen to reason.

A shout came from farther down the lake as two security officers emerged from the woods. They shook their heads and waved, signaling they hadn't found anything.

Cocoa watched them with anxious eyes, ears flicking back and forth.

A familiar bark cut through the tension.

Iris.

Gina appeared with her graceful collie in tow, winding her way down the grassy slope toward us. She gave me a quick nod, then focused on Luke. "I brought coffee," she said, holding out a thermos. "Thought you might need it."

Luke took it, murmuring thanks. Cocoa perked up slightly at Iris's arrival but made no move to greet her. He just sat beside Luke like a sentry, eyes on the divers. Iris, sensing his mood, kept her distance and lay down quietly a few feet away.

"Poor boy," Gina whispered, but it was unclear whether she was talking about Luke or Cocoa.

"He's taking it all in," I murmured. "I think he knows something's wrong."

More movement came from the path behind us. Carly arrived, out of breath, Bert at her side. He looked like he'd been crawling through brambles; his hair and clothing were dotted with bits of twig and burr.

"Anything?" she asked, glancing between us.

I shook my head. "Not yet."

"Bert's been helping in the woods with a few students. We did a full sweep of the ridge trail. Nothing."

Luke stared out at the water, jaw clenched. The divers had surfaced again and were chatting to one of the campus officers on the dock, their voices too low for us to hear.

I glanced at Cocoa. He was leaning so hard into Luke I thought he might topple him over. His tail gave one slow wag.

We stood like that for a while, silent, watching. The kind of silence that thickens with every second. Somewhere in the background, a duck quacked. A cicada buzzed. But all I could hear was the rhythm of my own breath and the occasional sigh from Luke beside me.

Then a sharp whistle split the air.

We all jumped and looked over to where one of the divers had surfaced. He was waving an arm in the air.

My heart sank.

We all waited for him to speak.

Eventually, he lifted his mask and shouted, "I've got something!"

Chapter 21

Accident or Murder?

"This can't be happening." Luke gazed at the still form of his friend lying on the lake bank, his face blank with shock.

Detective Maddox stood nearby, that no-nonsense air of authority practically radiating off him. Even Sheriff Grady had fallen in line, nodding at Maddox's instructions and scurrying off to carry them out. Under different circumstances, I might have found it faintly comical. Today, there was nothing funny about it.

The divers moved back, giving space to the paramedics. They were speaking in low tones, the sort of conversation you knew you weren't meant to overhear. I could see Carly watching too, holding Bert's hand as if steadying herself. Gina stood on my other side, Iris pressed close to her leg. Cocoa stayed glued to Luke, his big eyes flicking between Luke's face and the small knot of activity on the bank.

We all kept our voices low, as though anything louder would be disrespectful.

"He must have fallen in walking home," Carly murmured, not taking her eyes off the scene.

My heart went out to Luke, to Monty's family, to his friends who would be devastated by the tragic loss. "Unfortunately, it looks like it. It was dark that night... maybe he lost his footing."

"Maybe he drank more than he thought at the party," Gina whispered so Luke couldn't hear.

The word "party" felt almost jarring, like it belonged to another world. A world where Monty was still walking around campus, laughing with Luke, making plans for the weekend. They'd both been at that frat house on Friday night. According to Luke, Monty had left early after a fight with his girlfriend, Evie. It seemed impossible that a decision like that could end here, on this bank.

Luke had barely said a word since his friend's body had been retrieved from the water. His hands were thrust deep into his jacket pockets, shoulders hunched as though trying to make himself smaller. Cocoa nudged him gently, once, twice. Luke didn't look down.

The sound of footsteps on the gravel drew my gaze. Lindy Huang approached, her expression soft with sympathy. She stopped beside Luke.

"I'm so sorry for your loss," she said quietly.

Luke swallowed hard and nodded, but his eyes stayed fixed on Monty's body.

"Was it just a tragic accident?" I asked her.

Lindy glanced over at the paramedics, then back at us. "I shouldn't say too much," she said, lowering her voice even further, "but it looks like he has a head wound. Could be from hitting it when he fell in... or it could be from just before."

That drew our attention like a magnet.

"You mean..." Gina began, but Lindy gave a small shake of her head.

"I don't know," she said. "And I'm not the one who'll decide. But I thought you should be prepared... it might not have been an accident."

She gave Luke's arm a gentle squeeze, then stepped back toward the group by the bank.

The four of us stood there, silent for a long moment. The only sounds were the rustle of leaves overhead and the faint lap of the lake against the shore.

Carly let out a breath. "If it wasn't an accident..."

"Then someone was out there with him," I said.

I looked over at Luke, but he was staring into the water, tears slipping down his cheeks. Cocoa whined and leaned harder against him, as if he knew exactly what was needed.

The sun dipped a little lower, casting the lake in a wash of soft gold that felt cruel in its beauty. Somewhere behind us, a bird sang its evening song. Life carrying on, but as we stood there, I wondered if the cause of Monty's death had been something far more sinister than a drunken misstep in the dark.

To my surprise, Luke was waiting at the door of the Book Mark when I got there the next morning. "You really don't have to be here," I told him. "Take the day off. You've had a terrible shock." We all had.

He shook his head. "Tess, what if Monty was murdered too?"

I stared at him. The thought had been playing on all our minds, especially since Lindy's shocking reveal about the head wound.

"We don't know that for sure," I cautioned. It would be

wrong to start jumping to conclusions, especially with such a sensitive subject. Monty's parents would be going through all kinds of hell right now, along with his girlfriend and his friends. Luke included. "He could have hit his head when he fell in."

"There aren't any rocks on that side of the lake," Luke insisted. "I checked."

He'd been busy.

I unlocked the front door and we went inside, Luke still babbling. "What if someone followed him after the party and attacked him?"

I frowned. "Do you have someone in mind, Luke?"

"Well, he was fighting with his girlfriend."

I shook my head. We had to be very careful about casting suspicion on innocent people, especially students. They were young, they had their whole lives ahead of them. Something like this could be incredibly detrimental.

Still, we couldn't discount it either.

"What were they arguing about?"

"She felt he'd been neglecting her lately. I heard her say he was so wrapped up in his thesis that he didn't have time for her anymore."

"Was it true?"

Luke raked a hand through his hair. "Yeah, I guess. He was distracted, even I noticed that, but I thought that was just down to his workload."

I massaged my temples. The beginning of a headache was forming, and the day had barely begun. "Could he have been worried about something else?"

"Maybe. I don't know. I think I'm going to have another look around his dorm."

"I'm sure the police will be doing that," I pointed out.

"They think he was drunk and toppled into the water," Luke scoffed. "I know Monty. Firstly, he didn't ever drink that much, and secondly, he was sober when he left that party. I saw him go. He wasn't drunk."

I laid a hand on his arm. "Okay. I must admit it does sound suspicious. Where is Evie now?"

"In her dorm, I guess."

"Can you go and get her? Bring her here so we can have a word with her. It might pay to find out what she knows. Not because we suspect her of harming him, but because she might know why he was so distracted lately."

Luke nodded. "Then I'll go and look around Monty's dorm room."

"Just be careful," I admonished. "We don't want you getting into trouble with the cops."

"I will."

And with that, he took off, leaving the bell above the door jangling in his wake.

Chapter 22

The Bend In Pine

I folded my hands on the table, trying to keep my voice gentle. "Luke said you knew Monty really well. We're just... trying to understand if anything was bothering him lately. Anything apart from the thesis?"

Her gaze flicked to Luke before settling on the latte cup between us. "Not that I knew of." A pause. "Well—" she let out a breath, almost a laugh but not quite—"just me, I guess."

Luke shifted uncomfortably. "Evie—"

"No, it's fine," she said quickly. "I just... I gave him a hard time Friday night. I regret it now." Her voice caught, and she tucked a strand of blond hair behind her ear, the green streak catching the light. "He was so different lately. Distracted. Forgetful. He even forgot our anniversary, and Monty never forgets things like that."

"You think something was bothering him," I said.

"I think..." She trailed off, searching for the right words. "I

121

think there was. But I didn't see it at the time. And I'm a psych major, which is kind of pathetic."

"People hide things," I said softly. "Even from the ones closest to them."

For a moment, we all listened to the hiss of the espresso machine and the quiet shuffle of pages from the back of the store. Then I leaned in a fraction. "Did you stay at the party after your fight?"

Her eyes widened, as if she'd only just realized where I was heading. "For most of the night, yeah. It was like a sleepover."

"What time did you leave?"

She thought for a moment. "Around five, I think. Just after Monty."

"You walked home?"

"Yes. Along the road." She hesitated. "A friend walked with me part of the way."

I kept my tone casual. "What's your friend's name?"

"Lara Benton. She's in my Abnormal Psych class. We live in the same dorm."

I nodded, tucking the name away. "Thanks, Evie. That's helpful."

She gave me a small, wary smile, as if unsure whether she'd just confessed something important. I returned it with what I hoped was reassurance, all the while thinking I'd need to have a little chat with Lara Benton. Sooner rather than later.

Abnormal Psych let out just before noon. I'd timed it so I could intercept Lara before she disappeared into the swarm of students heading for lunch. I locked up the shop, hung a "Back in 10 Minutes" sign in the window—something I almost never do—and grabbed Cocoa's leash. He wagged at the prospect of an outing, oblivious to the fact that this was business, not pleasure.

The air on campus was warm and heavy with the scent of cut grass. The college was all red-brick buildings with white trim, black shutters, and broad granite steps. Towering maples cast generous pools of shade across the campus green, their leaves shifting lazily in the light breeze.

Clusters of students lounged on the grass or perched on the low stone walls, books and iced coffees at their sides. The white steeple of the chapel rose above the rooftops, bright against the deep blue of the summer sky.

I spotted Lara coming down the stone steps of Wentworth Hall, hugging a thick binder to her chest. Her honey-blonde hair was tucked into a knitted headband, and her cheeks were flushed from the cold. I intercepted her, and she stopped short.

"Lara?" I asked in a friendly tone.

"Yeah." Her clear blue eyes narrowed.

"I'm Tess," I said, "and this is Cocoa."

She smiled at the dog, as I'd hoped she would. Cocoa, I was discovering, was a great conversation starter. He put people at ease.

"I'm a friend of Luke's; he works with me at the bookstore."

She gave a hesitant nod.

"I spoke to Evie about last Friday night," I added. "I was hoping to talk to you too. It's important."

Something in my tone must have told her I wasn't here for casual chit-chat. She glanced toward the stream of students filing past, then stepped off the main path toward one of the quieter walkways. "Okay. What do you want to know?"

I fell into step beside her, Cocoa trotting between us. "Evie said you walked home with her on Saturday morning after the frat party."

"Yeah." Lara nodded, frowning a little. "She was upset

because she'd had an argument with Monty. We walked together part of the way."

"At what point did you split?" I asked.

We'd reached a bench under an old elm, and she stopped there, shifting her binder to her other arm. "You know the bend in Pine Street, just past the student union?"

"Yes," I said. I knew it well. It curved away toward the older part of town, while the straight stretch led toward the campus residences.

"I turned off there toward Mason Hall," she said. "Evie kept going down Pine toward her place."

"And that was the last you saw her?"

She nodded. "Yeah. She was pretty cut up. She said she was thinking about breaking up with him."

I studied her for a moment. Lara didn't seem evasive, just thoughtful, and maybe a little regretful. But if that was the point they'd parted, it meant Evie had walked alone for the rest of the way. And that stretch of road... well, it wasn't exactly bustling in the early hours of Saturday morning.

"Thanks, Lara. This helps."

"Is something wrong?" she asked carefully.

"I don't know yet," I said. And that was the truth.

Back at the shop, I headed straight to the map on the study table. Cocoa curled up on the rug at my feet.

Running my finger along Pine Street, I traced the route from the frat house to the bend Lara had described. From there, it was a straight shot toward the lake.

Chapter 23

She's Not The Type

"So what are you saying?" Carly asked me later that day. She and Gina had come over after work, and we were sitting around the study table, iced coffees in hand, staring at the map. "That Evie went after Monty and whacked him on the head?"

"She'd have to have pushed him in the lake," Gina added, leaning back in her chair.

"No, of course not." I took a breath. "I'm saying she could have."

Luke still wasn't back. As far as I knew, he'd gone to search Monty's dorm room again before heading to lectures. Even in grief, he couldn't afford to fall behind—something I admired, though I wished he'd let himself stop for air.

"Think about it. They had a fight, he was upset and stormed off. Then, she left with her friend Lara, who walked with her along Pine Street to the bend, and then they split up.

Lara went to her dorm, leaving Evie alone. She could have quite easily run down this lane—" I traced the route with my finger—"through the woods, to the lake, and intercepted Monty on the path."

Gina shook her head. "I don't know, Tess. She'd have to have timed it just right."

"He might have already passed, and she crept up on him," I said, my mind spinning through grim little possibilities. I really did need to stop reading so many gothic mysteries; they planted seeds in my imagination that sprouted far too easily.

Carly pursed her lips, her eyes softening a fraction. "I know Evie. She doesn't seem the type to suddenly decide to murder her boyfriend, even if he was being distant. She had the opportunity, I'll give you that, but not the motive."

"Yeah, I know." I sighed, eyeing the map's narrow road to the lake. They were right. This didn't feel like something the girl I'd spoken to that morning would do—too level-headed, too... contained. "But if she didn't, then who did?"

"Who's to say anyone did?" Carly reasoned. "It may have just been a tragic fall."

"He wasn't drunk," I reminded her. "Luke saw him leave. Perfectly steady, just upset. You don't topple into a lake unless you're inebriated—or something else is going on."

There was a silence as we all sat there contemplating this.

The door burst open with a frantic jingle of the bell, and we all jumped, but it was only Professor Riley.

"Good afternoon," Riley announced, shooting me one of his charming smiles. "Tess, I was wondering if I might speak to you about arranging a book signing for *Through the Canopy*."

It took me a moment to catch up. My thoughts were still tangled in my earlier conversation about Monty, and Riley's words seemed to drift in from a parallel, much less urgent world. "Oh—er, yes," I said, fumbling for a response. "I'm sure we can set something up."

Privately, I wasn't convinced how much draw it would have beyond the botany students. Then I remembered Monty was one of them.

"But it won't be for a while," I added gently. "Not until the town's had a chance to recover. I imagine your students must be very upset."

Riley inclined his head with grave deliberation. "Of course. The whole department is devastated by Mr. Alexander's passing. Such a promising young scholar." He shook his head and pushed his glasses up his nose.

It startled me to realize I'd never actually known Monty's last name until that moment.

"He was in your class, wasn't he?" Carly asked.

"That's correct. Such a bright young man. His death is a tragic loss to us all."

I swallowed against the knot in my throat, blinking back tears. "If you'll leave me your number, I'll call you to arrange the event once things have... quietened down."

"Of course." He reached into his jacket pocket and extracted a cream-colored card embossed with his name in elaborate script. "I look forward to your call."

He placed it on the counter, offered the room a parting nod, and took his leave. He hadn't been gone long when Luke rushed in, cheeks flushed from the exertion—and something more urgent.

"Now the police are saying Monty committed suicide."

"What?" I pushed my chair back, the legs scraping against the floor. "That's ridiculous."

"According to Lindy Huang, toxicology showed almost no alcohol in his system. They've decided he was so stressed by his thesis that he drowned himself."

"It's incredibly hard to drown yourself," Gina said reflectively.

We all turned to her.

"What? It's true. I've read about it. Your body's natural defenses kick in. You can't just will yourself to stay under. You'd have to be drugged or unconscious for it to happen."

"And Monty was a good swimmer," Luke said firmly. "He'd never be able to drown himself."

"What about the bump on his head?" I asked. "Aren't they considering that as proof of an attack?"

Luke sank into a chair. It was then I noticed he had an unfamiliar sweatshirt draped over his shoulders. He hadn't been wearing it when he'd dashed out of here earlier. Monty's, maybe? "I don't know."

I frowned. Maybe I should have another chat with Detective Maddox. He'd never come back after I'd asked him to look into Monty's disappearance, and I had the distinct feeling this case was slipping into the "open and shut" category—one they could box up neatly and file away without too many questions.

"Did you manage to take a look around his dorm room?" I asked.

"Yeah, but I didn't find anything. I took a ton of photos, though; they're all on my phone."

"What of?" Gina asked.

"Everything that was left scattered around—his work on his desk, the clothes on the floor, general ones of his room." He shrugged. "I don't know if it'll be any use, but Lindy taught us to be thorough and photograph everything just in case."

"She probably meant at a crime scene," Carly murmured, but I nudged her with my foot under the table.

"That's good work, Luke," I told him. "Forward them to me. A second pair of eyes might help."

He gave me a grateful half-smile.

"I'm going back to the lake," he said.

I swear, that boy had ants in his pants. I got that he wanted to do something to help solve his friend's murder—if it was a murder. I understood; doing nothing made you feel useless.

"Okay, fine," I said. "It's a quiet afternoon, so I can manage. Take Cocoa with you. He's good company."

And I meant it. Somewhere along the way, Cocoa had stopped being Henry's dog and become part of my little makeshift family, right alongside Luke, Gina, Carly, and Bert. The thought gave me a small, warm pulse of comfort, even against the day's grim backdrop.

"Come on, Cocoa," he called, grabbing the dog's leash. We all waved goodbye as he left the bookstore, dog in tow.

Chapter 24

A Race To The Finish

Cocoa

Walks. I had to admit I loved walks.

This guy... Luke... he was better at walks than Tess. Not that I minded when Tess walked with me, but I didn't have to hold back so much with Luke. It wasn't always easy to walk a human; they tended to trip a lot, and I had to watch for that.

What really surprised me was that they didn't keep stopping to sniff things. I mean, we were walking through grass and trees and a lake and all sorts of wonderfully smelling stuff. I swore I could smell squirrel. There must be one around here somewhere, but I wasn't sure where.

I wanted to follow the scent, but Luke kept calling me back to the trail, so I got distracted. If I saw one, though, I was going for it. Luke could be on his own for a minute or two.

Except... maybe I shouldn't.

I had failed Henry. I'd left him alone and look what had

happened. I mean, yeah, I knew I wasn't allowed in the kitchen—he had made that really clear—but it still felt like I'd let him down.

Squirrels suddenly didn't feel quite so important anymore. My tail dropped. I sighed.

Who was a good boy? Not me, that was for sure.

It was warm today, but there was a breeze coming off the water. I trotted beside Luke, ears bouncing, tongue flopping out the side of my mouth. Luke was quiet. Not the good kind of quiet, like when you were watching squirrels and plotting your next move. The heavy kind, where his steps felt slower.

As we walked toward the water, I had to admit to a certain disappointment. I was really, really hoping he would throw a stick like Tess did. If he could get it further into the water, that would be fun. I glanced back, but he just kept looking around like he'd lost something. It occurred to me that he was probably searching for squirrels too. Luke understood the danger of squirrels. How could he not? I got that. Good boy, Luke.

I left him to it as I picked up another scent. Iris's. It was old, but I liked that it was there. Maybe from our walk together? No, fresher than that. She had been here since then. I paused, thinking about her. Walking with her had been wonderful, and I was pretty sure I'd impressed her with my swimming skills. She'd smiled when I shook myself all over Tess. Tess had certainly made a strange noise, and Iris's human had definitely laughed. If you could make a girl smile, you were halfway there.

Luke was standing still, so I took my time and had a good sniff around. It was like he was on high alert. Maybe it wasn't squirrels. Maybe there was something else. Something he hadn't told me about.

I headed back, trying to figure it out. He looked so sad that I jumped up, landing with my front paws on his leg—just to let him know he was safe with me. I wouldn't fail again.

He didn't seem mollified. In fact, he stepped backwards, gave a little growl, and brushed his leg where I had landed. Something about mud, though I didn't really catch it.

Slapping his thigh, he called for me to follow him. I hated leaving Iris's scent. I wanted to roll in it, get it on my fur so I could sniff it later, but he had moved on now, so I wagged my tail and we continued our walk.

I decided to stay close to him. He was so distracted, he'd probably have walked into a tree if it wasn't for me. That was alright, though. I could sacrifice a few sniffs for his sake. He was a nice guy.

Eventually, he headed for a bench and sat down heavily. He wasn't looking around now, but I could tell he still wasn't happy. Whatever he'd been looking for, it wasn't here. I didn't know what to do for him. How could I cheer him up? I didn't even have my chicken to give him.

I hopped up onto the bench next to him and stared at him for a long moment. His head was in his hands, and he was staring at the ground, or maybe at his feet. Either way, I could feel his sadness and frustration.

There wasn't a lot that I could do, so I leaned in and licked his cheek. He lifted his head but didn't pull away. Some humans didn't like my kisses, but Luke turned to face me. I could tell his mood was a little better, so it had helped. Maybe if one kiss helped, a thousand would bring back his happiness.

I moved in and started licking his face like I was saving him from drowning. I was still expecting him to pull away, but then he did something I didn't expect. He hugged me.

Normally, I wasn't too comfortable with hugs. They made me feel as though I was trapped. With Tess, it was different. Even kind of nice. Surprisingly, it was the same with Luke.

I laid my head on his neck as he held me. My paws rested on his legs, but he didn't complain about the mud now. He just slowly stroked my head and gave me the occasional ear scratch. That ear attention was one of the best things about humans.

He was murmuring now, but I couldn't work out if he was talking to me or himself. I had no idea what he was saying because I wasn't really listening all that well, but I could tell he needed me, and I was happy to be there for him.

I wasn't only security; I also provided therapy. Usually, I made people laugh, but this was alright too. I think Luke was feeling better. He felt less bristly, less panicked. As I lay there, being petted, I thought what a nice way it was to pass a warm afternoon.

I still kind of wished I had my chicken, though.

The lake was busier than usual. We watched the humans in bright vests, talking in serious tones, and carrying ropes and things that clanked. Others were dressed head-to-toe in white and were scurrying around the trees and shrubs. I just knew they were searching for squirrels, although Luke's shoulders tightened when he looked that way.

After a bit, the breeze picked up, and Luke pulled on a sweatshirt that had been draped over his shoulders. Not his sweatshirt. I could tell because it smelled different.

Then, with a heavy sigh, he got up. I jumped off the bench, and we walked on. The path curved near a cluster of bushes, and my nose twitched.

Oh-ho, what was this?

I darted into the greenery, rummaged around for a while, and came up with something leather, soft and worn. It had the same smell as the sweatshirt.

Luke froze. He took it from me and stared at it for a very long time.

Then he yelled, "Good work, Cocoa. Excellent work! Good dog. Brilliant dog."

My heart swelled with pride.

Luke straightened, shoved the glove into his pocket, and without another word, started running.

Woo-hoo! A race!

I launched after him, legs stretching, ears flapping, tongue lolling joyfully. This was great. I didn't know why we were running, but whatever the reason, I wasn't letting him win without a fight.

We tore down the path, past the ducks, past the benches, the breeze roaring in my ears. We didn't stop until we reached the street, then the bookstore. I thought I'd won, but I couldn't be sure. It was close.

Chapter 25

Foul Play

"You found this by the lake?" I stared at Luke, then down at the glove, then back at Luke again.

"Cocoa did," he said, rubbing the dog's head. Cocoa looked very pleased with himself. They were both panting, like they'd just run all the way here from the lake. "It's Monty's, no doubt about it."

"One glove," I said thoughtfully. "I wonder if he was wearing one when they pulled him out of the water."

Luke cringed, and I regretted my crudeness. "Sorry, I mean when they found him."

He gave a little nod, then pulled out his phone. "We could ask Lindy."

"We should call Detective Maddox." He'd definitely want to know about the glove.

I filled up Cocoa's water bowl and left him lapping noisily

while I went into my office to call Maddox. He didn't answer, so I left a message on his voicemail.

When I came back, Luke was sitting at the coffee bar, the glove on the counter in front of him. "He was wearing the other one when they found him," he said, his cheeks still flushed from the run back. "Lindy confirmed it."

"Right." I frowned. What did it mean? One glove.

He glanced up at me. "This proves Monty didn't commit suicide."

I nodded slowly, coming to the same conclusion.

"I mean, who commits suicide with one glove on?" he continued. "You just wouldn't, would you?"

I wouldn't at all, but I got the point. This, and the bump on the head, clearly indicated foul play.

"Monty was murdered," I whispered. "No doubt about it."

It was past closing, so I shut up the store and flipped the sign on the door to "Closed." Detective Maddox still hadn't returned my call. I was getting pretty darn annoyed with him. Here we sat with valuable information and couldn't pass it on. All the more reason to keep investigating this ourselves.

"I wonder if the police are making any headway," I said, stifling a yawn. Luke looked washed out. Even Cocoa was snoring away on his bed. I still hadn't given him supper, so we needed to get home.

"Who knows?"

I couldn't blame him for losing faith. Mine was teetering badly. I'd had high hopes for Detective Boston, but it seemed he was as ineffectual as the sheriff.

"Let's call it a day," I said, getting up. "I need to get home and feed Cocoa."

He gave a lackluster nod. "Yeah, okay."

We let ourselves out, and I locked up, pulling the door firmly closed behind me.

. . .

I was just about to go to bed when the doorbell rang. Cocoa leaped up from his bed—the old one we'd taken from Henry's, not the new one, which was now at the bookstore in my office but had hardly been used—and barked.

I frowned and glanced at my phone lying on the coffee table in front of me: 10:05 p.m.

Who was visiting me at this hour?

Cocoa got to the door first and sniffed under it. His bark changed to an excited whine, so I wasn't too concerned. "Who is it?" I called.

"Detective Maddox," came the deep reply.

I froze. For some reason, my hand flew to my hair and whipped out the scrunchie, then I shook my head to loosen the tendrils, before hurling the circle across the room, behind the couch.

We'd unpick that one later.

I unlocked the door and opened it. "Detective. Bit late for a house call, don't you think?"

He gazed down at me. "You called me."

It's true. I had.

I stood back to let him in. "You'd better come in, then."

He stepped inside my apartment, and suddenly the room felt much smaller.

"Let's sit down, Detective. I've got a lot to tell you."

I sat on the sofa, and he eased his muscular frame into the armchair opposite me. "You mentioned you had found something that belonged to the victim in the lake?"

I nodded, got up, and fetched the clear plastic bag that we'd put the glove in. Returning, I handed it to him. "I'm afraid it's got dog drool all over it, and Luke's fingerprints, but that's Monty's glove. I believe he was wearing the other one when he was found."

Maddox gazed at the glove, then up at me. "How do you know—?"

"Lindy Huang is Luke's forensic science tutor."

He frowned. "She shouldn't be discussing the details of the investigation."

"We were there when you retrieved his body from the water, Detective. Anyone could have seen he was wearing a glove." I didn't want to get Lindy into trouble.

He grunted. "I suppose." But he wasn't happy about it.

"Anyway, that kind of rules out suicide, don't you think?"

He stared at me. "What makes you say that?"

I gave him an *Are you kidding?* look. "Who kills themselves wearing only one glove?"

He shook his head. "Victims of suicide are rarely thinking rationally when they... you know."

"Well, even in that state of mind, I don't think anyone would try to drown themselves with one glove on. By the way, did you know Monty was a good swimmer? He used to be on the swim team." That was a new bit of information Luke had given me. "There's no way he'd have drowned in that lake."

"With a head wound, he may have. If he was woozy or concussed, he could have easily slipped and fallen in."

That was true.

"I thought the head wound was recent. Didn't it happen just before he died?"

I got another dark stare, as if he was trying to make me out. "How come you know so much about police procedure?"

I was surprised by the sudden change in direction of the conversation, but I answered anyway. "My uncle was a Boston cop. Twenty-five years on the force. He used to tell us stories when he came round for supper."

A beat passed, then he asked, "What was his name?"

"Frank. Frank Winslow."

A flash of recognition sparked in his eyes. "I knew him. He was a good cop."

"I know." Uncle Frank was great. I hadn't seen him since I'd left Boston, but we were close.

"My mother always used to say I was more like my Uncle Frank than my own father. He was an accountant."

His eyes crinkled. "I can see that."

I paused, wondering why I was telling him this. I didn't usually offer up personal bits of information about myself to near strangers. Maddox just had a way of getting this stuff out of me.

"Anyway," I said, clearing my throat. "Let's get back to the glove."

He held it up. "Thanks for this. We'll get it analyzed and see what it comes back with."

"If he was attacked and it came off in the struggle, it might have the killer's DNA on it."

"If he was attacked, then yes. It's possible."

At least he'd agreed that much.

"Was that it?" he asked, his gaze shifting to a spot on the floor. I realized he was looking at my scrunchie. Somehow, I'd missed the couch, or it had rebounded off it, and now lay in the corner of the room. I ignored it, although I could feel my cheeks heating up.

"No, actually. There's more." A lot more.

He settled back down again and waited for me to elaborate.

"It's about Henry," I began, which got those dark eyes back on me. "Did you know he left a will?"

Maddox frowned. "Of course we knew. His lawyer told us about it when we questioned him."

Of course. That was a logical step.

"Well, did he tell you that Henry told him he'd left the bakery to a mysterious third party?"

A nod. "We were aware; however, without the actual document, nobody is going to inherit anything."

I nodded. "Have you talked to Peter Lane?"

He frowned. "Who's he?"

"Peter Lane is a restaurateur and amateur property developer in Maple Ridge. He owns Flint + Flame, the steak restaurant at the end of Main Street."

"How is this relevant?" He didn't mention whether he knew or had been to the restaurant.

"Peter wanted to buy the bakery. He made Henry an offer, but Henry turned him down."

Maddox shook his head, but I could see his jaw popping. He was annoyed he hadn't had this information sooner. Well, it wasn't like I hadn't tried.

"I wasn't aware, no."

"I saw a letter from him in Henry's things. It's still there at Henry's house if you want to see it."

He studied me, and I got the feeling he was trying to figure me out. "I take it you've spoken to Peter Lane about this?"

I smiled. "Good guess."

He smirked. "You're definitely your uncle's niece."

I would take that as a compliment.

"I don't think Peter is a viable suspect, if that's what you're thinking. He's the one who told me about the will. There was no chance of him buying Henry out if he'd left the bakery to someone else. Even without a will, the property would be tied up in probate for months. Henry's death doesn't benefit him at all."

"I'll still have to question him."

Fair enough.

He got up to leave.

"Oh, there's one more thing."

He shot me a frustrated look and sat back down again. "What now?"

"We met a man outside the alley leading to the bakery the other day. Buck Roberts, I think his name was. He said he used to work there with Henry years ago. That Henry trained him."

"So?"

"Well, weird that he should rock up now, don't you think?"

Maddox stared at me. "You're saying he's new to town?"

"Yes, he's from New York and staying in one of the B and Bs in town. I'm not sure which one. He didn't say." I pursed my lips. "He seemed like a nice enough guy, but I was wondering if he was this mysterious third party that Henry told his lawyer about."

"You think he's here hoping to inherit the bakery?"

I shrugged. "I don't know. Maybe."

"I'll ask him. We'll have to track him down."

"There are only a handful of B and Bs in Maple Ridge. It shouldn't be too hard."

"Thanks," he said, pushing himself up. This time I didn't stop him.

"You're welcome," I said, relieved to have gotten all this off my chest. "I've been wanting to tell you for a while, but..." I shrugged. "I've been busy."

"I know."

We stared at each other for a moment, and I felt a strange flutter in my stomach.

Maddox cleared his throat. "I'd better go. It's getting late."

I nodded and came to my senses. Whatever that was, I didn't want to dwell on it. "Of course. Thanks for stopping by."

"No problem."

I saw him out, making sure to avoid eye contact. Luckily, Cocoa had come to say goodbye too, so I had a good excuse. After I locked up, I stared down at my new friend. "Well, if that isn't the most unnerving man I've ever met, then I don't know."

Cocoa gave a soft whine of acknowledgment and rested his head against my knee. I patted him and then gave a loud yawn.

"What do you say we go to bed, buddy?"

He glanced up, and I could have sworn he nodded.

Chapter 26

You Have Got To Be Kidding!

A sharp bark jolted me awake.

I lay still for a long moment, the darkness pressing in, my heart pounding so hard it drowned out everything except the sound of my own breathing. For a second, I wasn't sure why I was awake. Then my fingers, fisted in the sheet, slowly unclenched as my mind caught up to what my body already knew.

The dog wanted a walk.

I exhaled, staring at the ceiling. "You have got to be kidding."

A *thump-thump-thump* rose from the carpet beside my bed. He was already there, tail wagging like a metronome set far too fast, panting in anticipation.

I didn't even have to look at my phone to know it was four in the morning.

"Seriously, I thought we'd discussed this," I told him. But I guess years of habit were hard to break. He was literally the definition of Pavlov's dog.

"Okay, just give me a minute to wake up," I muttered, pushing myself upright.

He wriggled all over, tail wagging hard enough to move his whole body. It wasn't like I had a choice anyway.

I sighed and surrendered to the inevitable.

Outside, the neighborhood lay wrapped in an eerie, pre-dawn calm. The air felt heavy, the sky still clinging to night's shadows. A quiet ache settled in my chest—the ache of knowing the one who should be here to take this walk never would again.

Cocoa, of course, didn't mind the dark spaces between streetlights. He trotted ahead, nose working furiously, as if the streets held secrets he was determined to uncover. It struck me that even though my house wasn't far from his old one, he seemed to be discovering it all for the first time. Maybe Henry had only walked him on certain routes—between his place and the Square, or along that lonely stretch by the lake.

It wasn't hard to be introspective when you were alone, waiting for a dog to do their business. I found myself thinking about Henry, about the bakery. Had he really wanted to leave it to someone else, or had he just said that to get Peter Lane off his back?

And who was Buck? The guy had just appeared out of nowhere, claiming to know Henry, but how did we know for sure that he did? Carly recognized his name but said he was nothing like the boy who used to work there. My suspicious mind began asking questions... Was it the same guy? Or had he known the real Buck and decided to take advantage of Henry's death, hoping to inherit? A con man, perhaps?

He hadn't come into the bookstore like he'd promised. Maybe I'd hunt him down too, have a little chat. It would be interesting to find out more about the flamboyant stranger.

I hoped Maddox would get to the bottom of it. A shiver passed through me at the thought of the burly detective, despite it being a mild summer's morning. Frowning, I kept walking.

I'd been so deep in thought I hadn't noticed Cocoa leading me straight down the path toward the lake. Suddenly, I halted.

"Oh, Cocoa. Do we have to go this way?"

He turned around, glanced at me, and gave a firm yap. That was a yes, then.

The lake was still, not a breath of air marring its glassy surface. Everything was tinged by a silver glow from the waning moon, and it would have been beautiful if not for the dreadful thing that had occurred here. I'd never look at that lake the same way again.

I yawned and glanced at my phone. It was twenty past four in the morning. I must be crazy to be doing this. Seriously, I had to break Cocoa of this habit; otherwise, I'd be walking around like a zombie all the time.

This was around the time Monty had drowned. He'd been coming back from that frat party on Friday night—no, make that Saturday morning. Hadn't Luke said he'd left around four?

It would have been a morning just like this one. Dark, still, not too cold. He'd have walked around the lake from the south side toward town. I glanced over to the spot where they'd retrieved his body.

Yes, it was clearly visible from here. The bend meant I had a perfect view of the path too. A chill went down my spine and I stopped walking. Cocoa halted beside me and shot me a questioning look, but my eyes were glued to the south side of the lake.

Was it possible?

No, it couldn't be. I was crazy to even think it... And yet, the thought wouldn't leave me alone.

What if Henry had seen whoever attacked Monty? What if he'd witnessed a murder?

My breath caught in my throat as the thought took hold.

It could have happened that way. Monty had died on the Saturday morning, even though his body had only been discovered yesterday.

The same morning Henry had been stabbed.

I scratched my head. Why hadn't we put this together before now? Two cases, two murders in the little college town of Maple Ridge. That was unheard of. It would make sense that they were linked.

I glanced down at Cocoa, who was still regarding me curiously. "Did you see who killed Monty?" I whispered.

He snorted through his nose and wagged his tail. That could have meant *Yes,* or *Can we keep going with our walk?* I wasn't sure.

Still, the thought gave me shivers. If Henry had seen Monty's killer, that changed everything.

Heart thumping, I slapped my thigh and turned around, striding off in the direction we'd come in. "Come on, Cocoa," I called. "We have to go home. I've got to call the others. I think I've just had a breakthrough in the case."

We all met at the bookstore at six o'clock. Admittedly, it was stupidly early, but I really felt this couldn't wait. Present were Luke, Gina, Carly, and Bert—and, of course, Cocoa. I stared at them bleary-eyed. Luke had made us all a strong black coffee, so our brains were kicking into gear, at least.

Gina had brought Iris, and she was curled up next to Cocoa on the rug, the chicken discarded between them.

"You're saying the same person who killed Henry killed Monty?" Gina asked.

"The other way around," Luke corrected. "Whoever killed

Monty killed Henry. Monty died first." He gulped and reached for his coffee.

"Think about it," I added. "Monty's attacker realizes Henry's witnessed their dastardly deed and sets off in pursuit. They follow Henry back to the bakery and knock on the back door."

Luke picked up the story. "Henry lets them in because he knows them, and while his back is turned, the killer stabs him with one of his own kitchen knives, leaving him to bleed out on the floor."

I closed my eyes, not wanting to imagine it. Trying to cut off the images before they flashed behind my eyes, but it was too late. I cringed and took a deep breath as I willed them away.

"That about sums it up," I croaked.

Carly had been listening, a thoughtful expression on her face. "I agree. That is certainly a possibility; however, didn't you say that Henry was killed around eight?"

"That's right, because I saved the peanut butter twists from burning."

Cocoa pricked up his ears at the sound of his favorite snack.

"If the killer followed him to the bakery, they would have gotten there around—?" Carly glanced at me. "What time did you say he went walking?"

My shoulders slumped. "They'd have got to the bakery around five in the morning."

"That doesn't necessarily mean it played out that way," Gina said, looking at us each in turn. "The killer could have recognized Henry. They didn't need to follow him because they knew where he worked. So, they waited until eight o'clock before visiting him at the bakery. Henry hadn't opened yet, so they didn't have to worry about customers or anyone seeing them."

"You're right," I said, perking up. "That's definitely possible. I mean, Henry let in his killer because the locks weren't tampered with. We know that much."

Luke drew in a ragged breath. "Right, so now we know how the killer did it and why. We just have to figure out who."

"That," I said, looking at him, "is the million-dollar question."

One Tough City

Come eleven o'clock, I'd had so much coffee to stay awake, my eyes felt like they were out on stalks. I was jittery too. I jumped like I'd been electrocuted when the door opened, jingling the bell.

"Didn't mean to startle you," a male voice said.

I turned to find Buck standing inside the door wearing jeans and a pale blue shirt with the sleeves rolled up, displaying his tattoos. He looked around, his gaze wandering over the shelves, the study area, and the coffee bar. "Wow. Fabulous place you have here."

"Thanks." I broke into a smile at the compliment. Cocoa sauntered over, curious, and gave Buck a good sniffing. "I was wondering if you'd stop by."

"It's taken me a while to get oriented, but I'm here now." He spread his arms and grinned.

Maple Ridge really wasn't that big a town.

"I've been walking around the campus." He bent down to scratch Cocoa's ears. Surely, the guy couldn't be all that bad if he liked dogs. "Very impressive. I just love all these quaint New England buildings, and that church steeple is magnificent."

"It sure is." I felt that way about the college too. It was beautiful and steeped in history. When I was getting the renovations done, I'd spent some time getting to know the town, and had explored the various facilities, buildings, and galleries. "Very different to New York."

He nodded. "That's for sure."

"Would you like a coffee?" I pointed to the shiny cream-and-chrome machine. Luke was attending classes this morning, so I was on my own. "I can make you one."

"Awesome. I'll have a hazelnut latte."

"Sure." I stepped behind the bar and got going on his order. He walked across the store, his blindingly white sneakers squeaking on the floorboards, and took a seat on one of the barstools while Cocoa followed, still sniffing.

"I actually just stopped by to say goodbye. I'm heading out tomorrow."

"Oh, really?" I glanced up. "How come?"

"There's nothing keeping me here anymore. I came to see Henry, and now he's gone..." He shook his head slowly. "I put it off for so long, and when I finally came... it was too late. Just one day too late."

"Why did you leave it so late?" I asked casually, pretending to be occupied with the machine.

"Oh, this and that," he said vaguely. I glanced up, eyebrow raised.

He sighed. "Okay, I may as well tell you. I've been trying to carve out a career for myself in New York, but that is one tough city. I started at the bottom but managed to work my way up to head baker at this gorgeous delicatessen on the Upper East Side. It's popular with all the celebs." He paused to take a breath. "But then—" He stopped.

"Then what?" I prompted, as the coffee machine gurgled. He had my full attention now.

"Then I got fired. Just like that, the boss let me go."

I frowned. "Wait, he fired you? Did he give a reason?"

"It was a misunderstanding. Some money had gone missing from the till, and he blamed me." His voice rose to a higher pitch, and his hands flew to his chest. "But I had nothing to do with it."

I didn't know whether to believe him or not.

He seemed nice enough, and he had a great sense of style, but was Buck on the level? Or was he just an opportunist playing us all, trying to get his hands on Henry's legacy?

I hadn't decided yet.

Cocoa, however, seemed to like him. He'd settled at his feet and was looking up at him, watching as he spoke.

"I'm sorry, that's a tough break." I pushed across the latte.

"Yeah. He said if I left quietly, he wouldn't call the cops." He reached for it with a nod. "Thanks."

If he really was innocent, that was an awful thing to have happened.

"So you decided to come up here to New Hampshire and see Henry."

"Yeah. He'd been my mentor when I was starting out, so I thought it would be fun to come up here and visit him. Maybe he'd even have some work for me."

Now I got it. "You wanted to ask him for a job?"

Buck nodded. "He'd helped me out before, so I thought maybe..." He sighed. "But I was too late."

I gave a sympathetic grimace. "When did you arrive? Sunday?"

He nodded. "That's when you saw me peering through the bakery window."

"Right. Did you drive up?"

"Nah, don't have a car. No point in the city. Thought I might try to find one here, though. I caught the college coach from New York. Took me seven hours."

I'd taken that coach into the city, so I knew what he meant. It was a long ride, but useful when you didn't want to drive. And let's face it, nobody wants to drive into Manhattan.

He sipped his latte. I contemplated another filter coffee but then thought I'd better not. I was already wired.

"When did you last speak to Henry?" I asked him.

He ran a hand through his hair. "Not for a long time. We kept in touch for a while after I left. You know, the occasional email and text message, but then we kinda lost touch."

How convenient. I still wasn't convinced, but I did know one way of proving it. "I don't suppose you know how to make Henry's peanut butter twists?" I asked.

He broke into a wide grin. "My gosh, I haven't made those since I was last here in Maple Ridge."

"But you remember how?"

His forehead wrinkled. "I think so."

"Great, because I used to order a batch from Henry every morning, and my customers are missing them. I don't suppose...?" I tilted my head and looked at him.

He laughed. "Sure, I can whip some up for you. Only problem is where. You don't have a kitchen here, I doubt the B and B will allow it, and Henry's is still off-limits."

"You can do it at my place. Tonight? After I finish work?"

"Deal!"

"Great, see you around six."

He left, and I turned to Cocoa. "So, buddy. Tonight we find out if Buck really is who he says he is."

. . .

"Who was that?" Luke said, walking in as Buck left.

"That is the guy claiming to be Henry's protégé."

Luke's eyes widened. "That's Buck?"

"Correct, and while he seems like a great guy, I'm going to put him to the test." I explained my cunning plan.

"Are you sure that's wise, Tess?" Luke said, frowning. "I mean, what do you know about this guy? He could be anyone."

"That's why I'm trying to prove he isn't," I argued. "Besides, Cocoa will be home. He'll protect me. Won't you, boy?"

Cocoa panted up at me, his tongue lolling to one side.

"Cocoa's more likely to roll over and let him pet him," Luke scoffed.

Cocoa gave a little yap of protest.

"You can come around too, if you're worried."

"Probably a good idea if I do," he reasoned. "I'll bring my books; I've got another midterm tomorrow." I knew Luke hadn't done much in the way of studying since Monty's death. It must be hard on him trying to keep afloat after he'd had such a shock.

"You know, you don't have to come in if you need to study," I told him. "I'll be able to manage for a week or so without you. Your exams must come first."

"I'm good," he said, and changed the subject. "What's Buck's story?"

"He got here on Sunday, the day after Henry died," I explained. "Caught the coach up from New York. Said he was devastated to have missed him. Henry was his mentor."

"Which we only have his word for," Luke pointed out, then he frowned. "Wait, did he say he got here on Sunday?"

"That's right."

"He couldn't have," Luke said, shaking his head.

"Why not?"

"The coach doesn't run on Sundays."

I stared at him. "What? Not at all?"

"Nope. That Buck lied to you. He couldn't have got here on Sunday, or if he did, it wasn't by coach."

Chapter 28

A Good Theory

"You did what?" Gina spluttered, coffee halfway to her mouth.

Luke had just finished telling her the story about Buck, and from the look on her face, she wasn't sure whether to scold me or stage an intervention.

"It seemed like a good idea at the time," I murmured, though even to my own ears it sounded more like a defense than a confession. My fingers played with the edge of a napkin, twisting it in a way that made Cocoa's ears perk up—he was always convinced a crinkle meant snacks.

"He might be a murderer!" Gina exclaimed, her voice pitching high enough to make Cocoa lift his head from where he'd been snoozing at my feet. He gave a sharp little huff, as if even he thought I'd lost the plot.

"That's what I said," Luke added, arms folded across his

chest, his brows knitting together in that steady, disapproving way of his.

I held up my hands. "Okay, but it's done now, so let's just see what he comes up with." I glanced sideways at Luke. "You'll be there, right? Studying. And Cocoa—" I reached down to scratch behind his ears—"will be on guard duty."

At the word "guard," Cocoa's tail thumped against the floor like a slow drumbeat. He didn't understand the context, but the tone was enough to convince him something important was afoot. His eyes gleamed with canine self-importance.

"I'm coming as well," Gina said, planting her elbows on the counter like she was staking her claim.

I sighed. "Really, it's not necess—"

"If he can cook," she went on, interrupting me, "I want some of those peanut butter twists."

I chuckled before I could stop myself. It felt good—a little pocket of warmth I didn't know I needed. "Fine. Six o'clock at my place."

The door jingled then, letting in a gust of cold air that smelled faintly of snow and just a hint of spice from the café down the street. In swept Lindy Huang with her usual brisk confidence, her long black hair coiled up into a bun and—unless my eyes deceived me—held in place with what looked like a pair of tweezers. I blinked. Tweezers? Only Lindy could make that work.

"Hey, Lindy. Can I get you something?" Luke called, and I caught the faint curve of a smile on his lips. It was the first I'd seen him give since Monty died, and it softened something in the air.

"That would be amazing, Luke. Thank you. It's been a hell of a day." Lindy slid onto a barstool, unbuttoning her coat in quick, neat movements. "I also have some news I thought you might like to hear."

The way she said it made me straighten. "What's that?"

"Henry Dawson's autopsy results came back, and guess what?"

The three of us froze mid-breath. "What?" we chorused.

"It turns out he was actually murdered much earlier than we thought. The ME put the time of death at between five and six o'clock that morning."

I felt my breath catch, like the words had stolen the air from the room. "No."

Gina blinked rapidly, as though struggling to process it.

Luke frowned. "I'm sorry, I'm confused. Did you say between five and six on Saturday morning?"

"Yes, correct."

Luke turned to me, his face pale, like the color had been rinsed away. "Then our first theory was right. The killer did follow Henry back to the bakery."

Lindy tilted her head. "What are you talking about?"

I drew in a steadying breath, the smell of coffee and old wood grounding me. "We had a theory," I explained. "Henry used to walk Cocoa every morning down by the lake on his way to work. He'd get in around five to start baking. Monty was killed around four-thirty that morning. At the lake."

As if on cue, Cocoa gave a small whine at the sound of Henry's name, leaning the weight of his solid, warm body against my leg. My hand found the soft ruff of fur at his neck, the comfort of that familiar texture calming me in a way nothing else could.

Lindy's eyes widened as she put the pieces together. "You think Henry witnessed Monty's murder?"

"That was our theory, yes."

"It's a good one." She looked between us, the café's coffee machine sputtering and steaming behind her like it was agreeing. "It works with the time of death."

"Not really," I said, the words heavier than I intended.

She frowned. "I don't understand."

"It's to do with the peanut butter twists," Gina cut in, her tone dry but her eyes sharp.

Lindy stared. "Nope, still not with you."

"I took them out of the oven," I said slowly, remembering the acrid curl of smoke in the air that morning. "When I found Henry, I called 911... and then took the twists out. They were burning."

Lindy's brow furrowed. "So?"

"So," I said, "they only take twenty minutes to cook. He must have been alive to put them in at eight o'clock. He couldn't have died before that."

The words hung in the air like frost clinging to glass.

Lindy shook her head. "Not possible. The body temperature and rigor showed he'd been dead for hours before you found him."

I closed my eyes for a moment, letting the timeline replay in my mind like a stubborn old film reel. It didn't add up—like a jigsaw with two pieces forced into the wrong place. When I opened them again, they were all staring at me. Even Cocoa was sitting now, ears forward, gaze fixed on my face like he, too, was waiting for the answer.

"If Henry was already dead," I whispered, "who put the peanut butter twists in the oven?"

A Killer Cook?

There was a long silence where we all just stared at each other, as though willing someone else to make sense of it first.

Carly's nose wrinkled. "Are we saying the killer made the peanut butter twists too?"

"They must have come back," Gina said finally, her voice quiet but certain. "It's the only possible explanation."

"Not so," Luke countered, leaning forward, elbows braced on his knees. "Most ovens these days have timers on them. He could have set it to start later, before you found him."

"Henry made them before he was killed," I tried, but the theory felt clumsy even as I said it. "And he put them in the oven to cook at eight."

"Henry did all his baking in the morning," Gina reminded me. "So everything was freshly made. If he'd set the timer for eight o'clock, he wouldn't have been able to bake anything else until then."

"Is that true?"

Luke shrugged, just as Carly gasped. "Buck is a baker. He'd know how to make the twists, wouldn't he? If he trained with Henry..." She looked at each of us, eyes wide.

I felt the color drain from my face.

"Who's Buck?" Lindy asked, brows drawing together.

"He's Henry's protégé," Luke said. "Just arrived in town, but we already know he lied about how he got here." He launched into the coach story, and I noticed Lindy's expression tighten the further he went.

I had to admit, it was looking more and more like Buck was untrustworthy. And I'd invited him into my house.

Lindy turned to me. "Do you think this Buck actually got to town earlier than Sunday? Early enough to kill Henry?"

I shook my head, my brain starting to throb from the mental gymnastics. "I honestly don't know what to think."

"But what about Monty?" Luke clawed a hand through his hair, making it even more disheveled. "I thought we'd decided Henry had been stabbed because he witnessed Monty's murder. That made sense to me. This..." He shrugged helplessly. "Not so much."

"I agree—it makes no sense at all," Gina said, her tone clipped.

"If Buck did arrive on Sunday, there's no way he killed Monty or Henry," I pointed out. "So maybe we should get the facts straight first."

"And how are you going to do that?" Lindy asked, narrowing her eyes.

That's when Luke told her what I had planned.

"You can't," Lindy hissed, putting a hand firmly on my arm. "Seriously, Tess. It's dangerous."

"It's too late," I said. "Besides, this will show us if he really does know how to make them—Henry's way."

"It's a good idea in principle," Gina allowed, "but in reality, we could all be killed."

"It would be three against one," I argued. Cocoa gave a soft yelp. "Make that four."

"Five," said Carly. "I'm coming too."

I looked at Lindy. "I suppose you want to be there as well?"

She managed a weak grin. "Wouldn't miss it for the world."

When Buck walked in that evening, he found the five of us sitting in the living room, waiting. The soft lamplight pooled in warm circles, though the air in the room was tight with unspoken tension. Cocoa bounded up immediately, greeting him with a slobbery enthusiasm that felt at odds with the lingering suspicion.

It still puzzled me how Cocoa could have taken such a liking to him—a possible killer. Then again, maybe my loyal companion wasn't the best judge of character.

Instead of looking anxious, Buck's face broke into a grin. "Oh, have I interrupted a party?"

He was looking very suave in a crisp white shirt, beige slacks, and a pair of black sports shoes polished to a mirror sheen. I had to admit, the man had style—though hardly baking attire.

"Word of the peanut butter twists got out," I said evenly.

He laughed. "Excellent."

Catching my doubtful glance at his clothes, he held up a canvas bag slung over his shoulder. "I brought my own apron, as well as some ingredients. Wasn't sure if you'd had time to get everything."

It had completely slipped my mind. "Oh, I'm sorry, Buck. I totally forgot to go shopping."

"Good thing I brought these with me, then," he said, setting the bag down on the table.

"I heard this is Henry's recipe," Gina piped up, stepping forward. "I'm Gina, by the way."

"Buck."

They shook hands. "And yes, Henry taught me how to make these, but as I told Tess this morning, it's been a while. I hope I can do him justice."

I met Gina's gaze over his shoulder. That remained to be seen.

"Let me show you where the kitchen is," I said, leading the way down the hall. The kitchen was bright under the fluorescent light, the counters bare and ready.

"Wonderful," he said, glancing around. "Now, if you just give me a bowl and some utensils, I'll get started."

I fetched what he asked for as he whipped out his apron. It was navy blue with a white insignia on the chest.

"Fernando's Delicatessen," I read aloud.

He grimaced. "Yeah, that's the place that fired me."

Now I had a name I could check out later. So far, at least, that part of his story held up.

I left him to it and rejoined the others. "Project Peanut Butter Twist is underway," I whispered.

Half an hour later, a warm, nutty aroma began to drift down the hall, curling into the living room and wrapping itself around us like a memory.

"It smells just like Henry's," Carly murmured.

It did.

I glanced around, noticing Cocoa's absence. I'd bet good money he was in the kitchen, working his own angle for scraps. Traitorous dog.

"I'd better go and check on him," I said, pushing myself to my feet.

"How do we know he's not going to poison us?" Carly whispered.

I gave her a look. "I doubt he's going to risk poisoning all five of us," I reasoned, though her words pricked uneasily at the back of my mind.

"How are you doing?" I called as I stepped into the kitchen.

"You're just in time," Buck said smoothly, sliding a tray from the oven. "These are done."

"Wow. They look amazing," I said honestly. "There are so many."

"I made double," he admitted, a mischievous glint in his eye. "You said your customers loved them."

"They do. Thank you."

"You're welcome. Shall I bring through a plate and you can sample the goods?"

I hesitated—just for a heartbeat—before nodding. "I'll do that. I really appreciate this, Buck. How'd you find the recipe?"

"Once I got started, it came right back. I may not have got the measurements exactly right, but I think they're close enough."

"They certainly smell good."

"I hope they taste as good as Henry's."

I forced a smile. "We'll let you know. I hope you're going to join us?"

That charming grin again. "Of course."

Well, that was something. He wouldn't poison us if he was going to eat them too... right?

Everyone looked up expectantly as I carried the plate into the living room, Cocoa trotting at my heels with shameless hope in his eyes. I set the twists down on the coffee table.

"I'll go first," I said, reaching for one. At the same time, I passed another to Cocoa, figuring he might sniff out anything suspicious. He inhaled it in one gulp—so much for that plan.

Everyone's eyes were on me, including Buck's, so I took a breath and bit into the pastry. It was—

Oh. My. Gosh.

Delicious.

"So good," I mumbled around another bite. That was all the encouragement anyone needed. The others dove in, and Buck waited until everyone had taken one before he picked up his own. I watched him take a generous bite, which eased something in my chest.

The room filled with murmurs of approval. Cocoa sat beside me, drooling, so I slipped him one more. "That's it," I warned. "I don't want you getting an upset stomach."

Buck laughed. "So, did I pass the test?"

We all froze mid-chew.

I cleared my throat. "You certainly did. I feel bad saying this, but these are almost as good as Henry's."

Chapter 30

I Love This Little Backwater

"He could have done it," Gina said once Buck had left.

"There's no denying he can bake like Henry," Carly agreed. "I believe Henry trained him."

Luke mumbled something through a mouthful of pastry that sounded suspiciously like "me too."

"I like him," I admitted after a pause. "It would suck if he turned out to be the murderer."

Cocoa, who had been snoozing under the coffee table, lifted his head and rested it on my lap as if to second my opinion. "You just like his baking," I told him, fondling one velvety ear.

Luke swallowed the last of his bite. "So, on the one hand, we believe he's telling the truth about Henry being his mentor. But on the other, we also know he could have stabbed

Henry in the back, made the peanut butter twists, and set the oven to start baking at eight o'clock."

"Knowing we would all assume Henry had been alive to put them in," I finished.

"It's fairly diabolical," Carly said with a little shiver.

"Murder usually is," I pointed out.

"What now?" Gina asked, glancing from me to Luke.

I told them about Buck's apron and the story he'd shared about getting fired from his job in New York.

"I can call them in the morning," Carly offered. "Find out if what he said is true."

"Thanks. I've got to place an order for new stock tomorrow, which will take up most of my morning." My mental list of new releases was growing by the hour, and I could already see the towers of unopened boxes waiting to be unpacked.

"Should we tell Detective Maddox?" Lindy asked suddenly. She'd been pretty quiet up until now, which meant she'd been thinking.

I hesitated. My gut said yes, but my conscience whispered —what if Buck was innocent?

"You have to tell him Buck lied about when he got here," Luke said, siding with Lindy. "He might be able to get the truth out of him."

I sighed. Of course he was right. "Okay, I'll call him tomorrow."

Lindy gave a short nod. "There might be a perfectly reasonable explanation for why he lied. In which case, Maddox will get to the bottom of it."

I studied her. "You rate him, don't you? As a detective, I mean."

She nodded. "I knew him back in Boston. We worked on a few cases together."

I knew Lindy had been with the Boston PD for years before moving here to teach, but she'd never told me why she'd left—just that she'd needed a change of scene. Like me, it seemed we both kept our personal histories carefully folded away.

"So, what's his story?" Gina asked. "Was he some big-shot detective over at Boston PD?"

"He used to be," Lindy said slowly. "Until one of his cases went south. It was a disaster—a drug bust gone wrong, if I remember correctly. His partner died. He blamed himself."

Luke let out a low whistle. "That's tough."

I didn't say anything, but it explained a lot—the seriousness, the gruff exterior, the guardedness.

"How long ago was this?" I asked.

"Must be six years now. I resigned just after it happened, but I remember because there was a bad fallout. Maddox even got suspended for a while, pending an internal investigation."

"Was he at fault?" I asked, remembering my uncle's grumbles about how easy it was to trip over red tape. How the paperwork could strangle a case before it even made it to trial.

"Sounds bad," Gina murmured.

"It was. I wasn't sure if he'd go back to the Force, but he did."

I arched an eyebrow. "Now he's out here, in Maple Ridge."

She gave a small, almost sad nod. "That's what happens after you fall from grace. You get sidelined, sent to all the backwater places." Then she grinned. "No offense."

"I love this little backwater," Carly said, huffing a bit.

"Me too," Gina chimed in.

And I had to agree.

True to my word, I called Detective Maddox as soon as I opened the next morning and told him about Buck lying about when he got to Maple Ridge.

"I'm not sure it's important," I admitted, "but you might want to ask him about it."

He said he'd look into it, though his voice gave nothing away.

Luke was manning the coffee machine like a pro, steam curling in the air as he kept pace with the morning rush. The plate of peanut butter twists Buck had baked last night was disappearing fast. I set my ordering list aside—there was no point trying to concentrate until the crowd thinned.

When the last customer left with a paper cup in hand and the final twist wrapped in a napkin, I told Luke I was nipping out for a sandwich and to keep an eye on things. His textbooks were stacked neatly behind the counter—he had a midterm this afternoon and planned to snatch study time between orders.

My first stop was Professor Riley's office in the science faculty's botany department. He was bent over his laptop, frowning in concentration, and didn't see me until I cleared my throat.

"Oh, Miss Holloway, I didn't see you there." He closed the laptop and pushed his glasses up his nose. "What can I do for you?"

"I'm looking for one of your PhD students—a Suzanne Morgan?"

"Suzanne, hmm..." He scratched his head. "I think you'll find her in the library. Our tutorial isn't until later, and she usually spends the day doing research there."

I thanked him and slipped out before he could start on another enthusiastic pitch for a book signing.

The Edward Palmer Library was hushed, the kind of quiet that made every footstep feel intrusive. I found Suzanne exactly where Professor Riley had said—at a wide desk, surrounded by an orderly chaos of stacked books and loose papers.

She looked up and smiled faintly. "Hey, Tess. What brings you here?" Her voice was low, though the place was practically empty.

"Sorry to interrupt, but I need to ask you something about Henry's oven. Do you have a minute?"

Her brow creased. "His oven?"

"Yes. I know it's a commercial bakery oven, but does it have a timer?"

"You mean a food timer? That counts down?"

"No, I'm talking about an automatic setting so the oven switches on by itself."

"Oh, you mean the delayed start? Yes. Henry set it every morning for his peanut butter twists."

My breath caught. "Was it set to turn on at eight o'clock?"

"Yes. How did you know?"

The real question wasn't how I knew—it was how the killer knew.

I shook my head. "It doesn't matter. Why did Henry use the preprogrammed setting?"

"Mornings were his busiest. He'd put the twists in, set the automatic start, and get on with prep for opening at nine."

"Did he do that every day?"

She nodded firmly. "Always. At least, for as long as I've worked for him."

"When did he prepare the trays?" I asked, picturing Henry in those final hours, wondering if he'd had them ready at five-thirty—right before the killer struck.

"I don't know exactly, but I'd guess after he'd done everything else."

"So not before six in the morning."

She shook her head. "Unlikely. Not with everything else he baked each day."

I thanked her and left her to her books, but my mind was already racing ahead. There were two possibilities: either

Suzanne was wrong and Henry had prepared the dough earlier, leaving the killer to simply pop them in... or the killer had baked them himself while Henry lay bleeding on the floor.

I shivered at the macabre thought. If it was the latter, then it was obvious who the murderer was.

As I walked past the bakery, the tape still in place across the front door, I had to admit, it was looking increasingly like Buck was the prime suspect. At this point, the young New Yorker would have a hard time proving he *didn't* kill Henry.

Chapter 31

A Twisted Killer

I hadn't been back long when the broad figure of Detective Maddox darkened my doorway. He had a habit of sweeping in with that purposeful stride, setting the bell over the door jingling, and then standing there—square in the entrance—scowling at me until I acknowledged his presence.

"Detective, how nice to see you again." I just managed to keep the sarcasm out of my voice. He didn't strike me as the type to take it well. "What can I do for you today?"

"I wanted to talk to you about Buck Roberts," he said, stepping further into the shop. I gestured toward the coffee bar. Luke had left for his midterm, so I was flying solo this afternoon, the hum of the espresso machine my only company.

"Why don't you sit down, and I'll make you a hot drink. On the house."

He nodded, though his eyes kept drifting as if following thoughts elsewhere.

"We can't locate him," he said, sliding onto a barstool and stretching his long legs out in front of him.

I moved behind the counter to make his coffee—black, if I remembered correctly.

"What do you mean you can't find him? He told me he's staying at one of the B and Bs in town. There are only three, I think." That was all I could recall offhand. I'd stayed in all of them when I'd first arrived, before I'd found my apartment.

"Well, if he's there, he's using a false name."

I frowned. That didn't sound like Buck. He'd once told us the story of his name and how it didn't suit him at all. He'd never made a secret of it, so what reason would he have to lie?

"What about out of town?" I asked, even though he didn't have a car. There were a handful of B and Bs and lodge rentals scattered in the surrounding countryside.

"Yeah, maybe." Maddox rubbed his jaw. I noticed he was looking a little stubbly, like he'd skipped shaving that morning. Maybe juggling two homicide investigations was getting to him. It had to be stressful—especially with only an inept sheriff and a rookie deputy to help.

"You sent the sheriff to look?" I asked. It would explain why Buck hadn't been found yet; the sheriff didn't strike me as the sharpest tool in the box.

"No, I'm not stupid. I sent his deputy. Good kid."

The corners of my lips twitched upward. At least he knew who he was dealing with. "That's good. I'm sorry I can't help you. That's all Buck told me."

Maddox sat at the bar, staring into the coffee I'd just set in front of him. I took pity. "I heard the time of Henry's death was much earlier than we thought?"

He grunted. "Between five and six in the morning."

"And that's indisputable, is it?"

He glanced up, eyes narrowing. "Yeah. Why?"

I reminded him about taking the peanut butter twists out of the oven. It took a moment for it to sink in, but then his eyes widened as the dots began to connect. Of course, he should have realized earlier, but a detail like burnt pastries wasn't important enough to make it into an incident report. By the time Maddox had taken over the case, it had been forgotten—its relevance lost.

I had mentioned it to him before, but clearly it hadn't stuck.

"I'm guessing they don't take three hours to cook?"

"No, sir. Twenty minutes or so."

He was quiet for a long beat, steam curling from his cup and ghosting across his face. When he finally spoke, his voice was rough. "How do you explain that, then?"

I put my hands on my hips. "Well, funny you should ask."

I explained about the automatic settings on Henry's commercial oven and his routine of starting the twists at eight o'clock sharp every morning, so they'd be ready just before opening.

"The killer must have known that," Maddox said, echoing the conclusion I'd reached in the library not long ago.

I nodded. "There's something else."

One of his eyebrows ticked upward.

"According to Henry's shop assistant, Suzanne, he didn't prepare the dough for the twists early. Certainly not before six o'clock."

He scowled. "But he was dead by then."

"Exactly."

He let out a long, low exhale. "This complicates things."

"On the contrary," I said. "It simplifies them. If Henry didn't make the twist dough before he died, there's only one explanation."

Maddox gave me a look like I'd lost my mind. "You're suggesting the killer made them?"

I tilted my head. "And if the killer made them, there are only two other bakers in town who could have done it. One, Sophie, you've already ruled out. The other you can't currently locate."

Maddox hissed out a breath. "Buck."

"The only part I don't get," I added, once he'd downed his coffee in one go, "is how this ties to Monty's death."

"How do you mean?"

I rubbed my forehead. "Buck had nothing against Monty. He didn't even know him."

"We don't know that," Maddox countered.

"True, but it's unlikely. We know Monty died on the lake path, which puts his murder before Henry's—sometime after four o'clock. Henry died between five and six, according to the ME."

Maddox nodded, but his gaze stayed locked on me.

"We also know Henry walked the lake path to work—between four and five—so it's probable he witnessed Monty's murder." I paused. "Which is why he had to die."

"A sweeping assumption," Maddox said, shaking his head. "We don't know for sure the murders are connected. You're also assuming Henry walked the lake that day. Maybe he took another route—or didn't go at all."

I scoffed. "Have you met his dog? He wakes me up at four o'clock. Every. Single. Morning. There is no way Henry didn't take him for a walk." I was one hundred percent confident about that.

Cocoa sauntered over and looked up at me expectantly. "Not right now," I said, fondling his ears.

Maddox slid his empty cup toward me and stood. "Well, we won't know for sure until we bring him in. I'm putting out a BOLO, and when I get him in the interrogation room, he's got some explaining to do. Thanks for the coffee."

And with that, he swept from the bookstore, the bell over the door jingling behind him.

Chapter 32

The Hidden Thesis

Cocoa and I had just gotten home when Gina called for an update. She'd been busy all day and hadn't been able to stop by the store. While I was on the phone with her, Carly's name popped up on my screen, followed by Luke's, both calls sliding straight into voicemail.

I filled Gina in, then told her to pass the news along to Carly while I called Luke back. "Hey, how'd the midterm go?"

He gave a low, noncommittal sound. "Okay, I guess."

"I'm sure your professors will understand if you don't do too well," I said gently. "You've been through a traumatic experience."

"About that," he said, and I caught the murmur of voices and bursts of laughter in the background. He must have been in his dorm.

"What is it?" I asked.

"Something strange just happened," he said, and there was a tightness in his voice that made me sit up a little straighter.

"Oh, yeah?"

"I found part of Monty's PhD paper in my dorm room."

I frowned. "The one he was working on so diligently?"

"Yeah. It's the second half—about fifty pages' worth. I found it under my mattress when I was changing my sheets."

I was glad Luke was changing his sheets, but I couldn't fathom why Monty's thesis would be there. "Do you think he put it there?"

"I guess he must have. It's almost like... I don't know. It feels like he hid it there."

I was silent for a beat. Luke was right—you didn't stash something under a mattress unless you wanted to keep it hidden.

"Could it have fallen there by accident?" I asked, more to cover the bases than out of real belief.

"No way. This was right in the middle, between the bed slats and the mattress. It had to have been put there."

I frowned. "That is strange. Why would Monty hide his thesis under your bed? For safekeeping, maybe? Was he worried someone was going to steal his work or something?" I couldn't think of another reason it might end up there.

"Possibly. There are a few other students working on theses, but I don't know what theirs are about. I didn't pay much attention," he admitted. "I wish I had now."

"Maybe Evie knows why he felt he had to hide it?" I suggested.

There was a pause. "I'll ask her," Luke said. Then the line went dead.

I exhaled and ran a hand through my hair. It had been a long day, and I was well and truly pooped. I collapsed onto the couch and flicked on the television. Some procedural cop show filled the screen, but I wasn't really watching.

My thoughts kept drifting—more often lately—to Detective Maddox. The actor on the show could have been his TV double: tall, broad-shouldered, hunky, with that same chiseled jaw. I thought about what Lindy had told me—about the partner he'd lost. That kind of thing had to leave a mark.

I wondered if my uncle knew him. Uncle Frank had retired from the force now, but he'd had a long and respected career. It had been a while since we'd spoken. Maybe I'd give him a call.

I pulled up his number, hit dial, and set the phone on speaker beside me. Frank would be home now, probably watching TV too—he liked a good cop show as much as anyone.

Cocoa wandered over, sniffed the phone, and then curled up at my feet. He'd had his supper and was already drifting toward sleep.

The call connected, and Frank's voice boomed into the room. He'd always been loud—he claimed it was from years of shouting at bad guys. As a little girl, I'd believed him without question.

"Scooter! I thought that was your number flashing on my phone."

His childhood nickname for me still made me smile. "Hi, Uncle Frank."

"It's good to hear from you. What are you up to?"

"Oh, you know. Just running the bookstore. You should come visit sometime. Maple Ridge is a great place."

"Growing on you, is it?" His warm belly laugh rolled through the speaker.

"It is," I admitted. "How are you?"

We exchanged news for a while—roof repairs, the fact that he was seeing someone new. "Her name's Margo," he said, and he sounded genuinely happy. I was glad for him. My aunt

Sylvia had passed nearly ten years ago, and it was good to know he was getting out there again.

"I'm happy for you, Uncle Frank. You'll have to bring her up here for a weekend."

"Maybe we'll do that, Scooter. Now, what's the real reason for your call?"

He knew me too well.

"Can't I just phone to say hi to my favorite uncle?" I huffed, though we both knew better.

"Of course you can. And for the record, I'm your only uncle. But I can tell by your voice you've got a question."

I could see why he'd been such a good cop.

"Okay, I admit it—I do have something to ask you."

"Shoot."

"Do you know a Boston PD detective by the name of Maddox? Larsen Maddox?"

There was a pause. I could picture him scratching his balding head. "Yeah, I think I do... Yeah, it's coming back to me now. He's the guy who was involved in that drug bust that went bad. Major shootout. A cop lost her life."

"Her life?" Lindy hadn't mentioned his partner had been a woman.

"Yeah, it was terrible."

"Can you remember what happened?" I asked, though Lindy had already given me the basics.

"If memory serves, they'd linked this drug kingpin to multiple murders. A snitch tipped them off about a big deal going down and said the guy would be there. They were supposed to wait for the drug squad, but it looked like their suspect was leaving, so Maddox made the call to move in early. Let's just say it didn't work out well."

"How come?"

"They opened fire as Maddox went in. He took cover but

got pinned down. His partner, a rookie fresh to the force, tried to assist him..."

I held my breath, knowing what came next.

"She got hit. Didn't make it."

I exhaled slowly.

"By the time backup arrived, she was dead, and Maddox had been shot too."

"Maddox got shot?" I gasped. Lindy hadn't told me that part.

"Yeah, in the shoulder, I think. He had surgery and recovered, but I don't think he ever got over losing her."

"Was there an investigation?"

"Yeah. Internal Affairs got involved. Maddox was put on leave until it was done."

"What were the findings?"

"That he'd acted impulsively and, by doing so, had indirectly put his partner in harm's way."

"Yikes," I murmured.

"Yeah. He took some time off, then transferred to another division. That kind of thing sticks with you."

I was quiet, processing it all.

"Anyway, why d'you ask?" Frank said.

"Oh, there's been... an incident here, and he's the lead detective on the investigation."

"An incident? What kind of incident?"

I sighed. There was no point dodging the truth; Frank would ferret it out anyway.

"A murder," I said.

"A homicide?" His voice rose in surprise. "I thought you said Maple Ridge was a nice place."

"It is," I assured him. "This is... well, anyway, it happened, and now Detective Maddox is here questioning everybody."

"And you thought you'd get the lowdown on him?"

"I just want to know if he's capable."

"Oh, he's capable, all right. Before the drug bust, he was one of the most promising officers on the force. Best closure rate in homicide. Our paths crossed on a case once. I remember thinking he was good—but impatient and overly confident. I guess what happened humbled him somewhat."

Or just turned him into a grouch.

We chatted a bit longer before saying goodbye. I smiled as I set the phone down. It was good talking to Uncle Frank again. He was all I had left. We promised to arrange a visit soon—so I could meet this Margo in person.

Chapter 33

Peanut Butter Twist

Thanks to my early morning walks, I was in bed by ten o'clock. I couldn't keep my eyes open a moment longer. When Cocoa woke me up at four the next morning, however, I didn't feel nearly as groggy as usual. God forbid—I was actually getting used to this crazy routine.

Still, I took my time getting ready, so when we finally left the house, it was already half past. My cunning plan was to nudge our walk later each day until we hit six o'clock instead of four. Six, I could live with.

I'd learned Cocoa's habits by now. First, he'd lift his leg on the nearest lamppost, then on a tree, and finally on Mr. Hoover's picket fence. We'd even changed our route. Instead of heading to Henry's and then down to the lake, we cut through the back roads near my house until we came to a brook that eventually fed into the lake. A rugged little path ran alongside it, shaded by trees, carrying us most of the way.

Before we reached the point where it opened up, I stopped.

"Come on, Cocoa. Let's go get breakfast."

I was banking on the word breakfast to sway him. I couldn't stomach going down to the lake today. For once, I didn't want to think about what had happened there.

It worked. Cocoa turned—reluctantly, but without protest—and trotted back up the path toward me. We walked the mile home, and by the time we stepped inside, I felt surprisingly refreshed and more than ready for my first cup of coffee.

I got to the Book Mark early. Seven a.m. early. I blamed Cocoa. The silver lining was the extra time to finish the orders I'd put off the other day and get a start on the month's accounts. This getting-up-early thing was making me far too productive.

At eight-thirty, I felt a pang. That was when Henry would usually stroll in with a box of pastries. I'd make him coffee, we'd chat a bit, gossip about the other Main Street shop owners, and then he'd hurry back to the bakery.

"Oh, Henry," I whispered. Cocoa's ears flicked toward me.

I busied myself arranging the table displays and taking stock of supplies. The grocery list was growing—paper cups, lids, sweeteners. I was just setting out a stack of cups when frantic knocking rattled the front door.

I looked up and gasped. A man stood outside in a dark sweatshirt, the hood pulled low to shadow his face. Jeans, and the whitest sneakers I'd ever seen.

Buck.

He knocked again and pushed the hood back just enough for me to see his face. "Please, Tess. Please let me in."

I hesitated. I could call Maddox and have him picked up.

But there was something in his expression—raw fear—that made me pause. He was scared. Like, really scared.

Cocoa padded forward to stand beside me, gaze fixed on Buck. Oddly enough, he wasn't growling. Not a hackle raised. I trusted my dog.

Taking a deep breath, I opened the door.

Buck slipped inside and moved quickly out of sight of the windows. He hovered behind the bar, shoulders hunched, shivering—not from cold, but from fear.

"Buck, what on earth is going on?" I asked, watching Cocoa sniff his pant leg. I hoped he wasn't going to pee on it.

"The police are after me," Buck said, voice low and urgent. "They've been asking around the B and B. They want to take me in for questioning."

"Okay," I said slowly. "And why is that a problem?"

"Don't you see?" He wrung his hands. "They want to arrest me. They think I killed Henry."

I hesitated. "Did you?"

"Of course not!" His voice cracked. "Henry was my friend. My mentor. Why on earth would I kill him?"

I studied him, weighing my next move. This was as good a time as any to confront him. Emotional people sometimes told the truth they'd been holding back.

"I know you didn't come into town on Sunday," I said quietly. "The coach doesn't run on Sundays."

His eyes widened, and he slapped his forehead. "Duh. I'm so stupid. I didn't know."

"Why did you lie?"

He took a moment, then said, "I'll tell you, but only because I trust you, Tess. You've been nice to me since I got here. I'm hoping you'll believe me."

"Try me," I said, keeping my voice neutral. I was withholding judgment on this until I'd heard the full story.

"Okay. Well, I actually arrived last Thursday. I came to see

Henry, at his invitation. It had been a while, and I'd just lost my job, so I figured, why not?"

I stared at him. "Henry invited you?"

"Yeah, he left a message a couple of weeks back. Said it was time we caught up. He invited me up here."

"Do you still have his message?" I asked.

He shook his head miserably. "No. Like a fool, I deleted it."

I bit my lip. The police could check call logs to confirm contact, but they couldn't retrieve a deleted message's contents.

"What did Henry want?" I asked, going with it. For now.

"I went to the bakery. It still looked exactly the same." His eyes glazed over as he talked, remembering. "I helped Henry in the kitchen. It was like old times. It felt so... so right."

I kept quiet, letting him talk.

"That evening, back at his place, he told me he'd written a will. Said he had no living relatives, so he was leaving the bakery to me. And he asked if I wanted it."

My eyebrows shot up. "He asked you if you wanted the bakery?"

"When he retired, yeah."

I shook my head. "Why would he ask you that? Why now?"

Buck smoothed a hand over his hair. "I asked him that too. He said he was getting on and couldn't keep it up forever. He had a fishing cabin in the woods, and he wanted to spend more time up there."

That tracked. Henry was pushing sixty, and the bakery's hours alone were grueling. I thought of what Suzanne had said about the cabin and feeding the fish. Buck wasn't lying about that part.

"Okay, so you said yes. Then what?"

His eyes widened like a child about to open a gift. "I

couldn't believe my luck. It was like Henry was my guardian angel. He'd taken me on as a kid, when I'd had no prospects and my parents had kicked me out. Now here he was again, coming to my rescue."

I nodded. That was Henry all over. He was kind to the core.

"Why didn't you just tell me this from the start?"

"Because... well, you can see how it looks. Henry's murdered in his own kitchen, and here I am—a stranger in town—his sole beneficiary."

I had to admit, it didn't look good.

"I was scared if I said I'd been here since Thursday, everyone would think I'd done it. So I lied about when I arrived."

"Except now you've been found out, and you look even guiltier," I pointed out.

"I know." He hung his head. "I'm an idiot."

I took a breath and tried to think through the jumble of thoughts in my head. How could we prove Buck didn't kill Henry? "Do you have an alibi for between five and six a.m. on Saturday?"

"I was at the B and B, but there's nobody around at that time."

So no one to confirm whether he stayed put or not.

I pursed my lips. We needed more if we were going to get him off the hook. "Did you see Henry's will? Did he show it to you?"

"No, he just told me about it."

I hesitated, then said, "You probably don't know this, but Henry kept the only copy of his will. Nobody seems to know where it is."

"You mean it's l-lost?" he stammered.

I grimaced and gave a nod. "So even if what you're saying is true, there's no proof. Not without the will."

His face drained of color. "I'm going to prison, aren't I?"

I didn't admit that if he was, I'd be the one to have put him there. I'd literally told Maddox that it could only be him.

I bit my lip as a thought occurred to me. "Buck, were you with Henry on Friday as well?"

"Only in the afternoon, yes. I helped in the bakery again. He liked having me there."

I suddenly had a thought. "Did you help him prepare the peanut butter twists for the following day?"

He looked guilty. "How'd you know that?"

I broke into a grin. "Firstly, the ones you made at my house the other night were just too darn good. You'd have had to have done it before, and not fifteen years ago."

He gave a sheepish grin.

"And it explains why they were already made on Saturday morning. You stored them in the refrigerator, I'm guessing?"

"Yeah, Henry didn't like doing that, but it saved him having to make them first thing in the morning."

I walked around and put a hand on his arm. "Buck, you have to call the police and turn yourself in."

"What? No! I didn't do anything."

"I know that, but what you've just told me might actually save you from prison."

"Huh?" He was sweating now, a sheen glistening on his smooth forehead. "I don't understand."

"We thought the killer had made the twists on Saturday morning," I told him. "After Henry was murdered. That was the only explanation."

Buck looked at me like I'd lost it.

I glanced at the clock. It was nearly opening time. "Sit down, Buck. I need to tell you a story."

Chapter 34

You've Made Your Point

Maddox arrived a little after ten, a familiar scowl carved deep into his face. He pushed the door open with enough force to almost break the bell off, then strode inside like a storm cloud. Luke was manning the coffee bar, steam rising in lazy curls from the espresso machine, while I'd roped Carly into helping with customers so I could deal with the detective.

"What is it, Tess?" he barked. "I'm in the middle of a manhunt here."

"If you'll sit down, I'll tell you," I said evenly. I'd promised Buck I'd explain everything to Maddox first, so that when he took Buck into custody, he already had the full story. Less chance of misunderstandings that way.

He dropped onto a barstool, his dark eyes scanning my face with an impatient flicker, as if willing me to hurry up.

Luke slid a black coffee across the counter, earning a brief nod of thanks.

"It's about Buck," I began, then laid it all out—Henry contacting him, inviting him to Maple Ridge, their conversation, the news about Henry leaving the bakery to Buck, the years of mentorship between them.

"You know where he is, don't you?" Maddox guessed sharply. "You need to tell me, Tess, otherwise I'll have to arrest you for aiding and abetting."

"I will tell you," I said, keeping my tone reasonable, "but first I need you to listen. I want you to understand that Buck didn't kill Henry."

He gave me a hard stare. "What are you talking about? It was you who said—"

"I know what I said," I cut in before he could finish. "But I was wrong. Buck did make those peanut butter twists—I was right about that part—but he did it on Friday evening, with Henry, in the bakery kitchen."

Maddox dragged a hand through his hair, leaving it slightly mussed. "What?"

"Buck arrived in Maple Ridge Thursday afternoon. He went straight to see Henry, and that's when Henry told him about the will."

"That just proves he had motive," Maddox argued. "With Henry dead—"

"Henry wanted to make sure the bakery wouldn't be sold off and turned into condos like Peter Lane wanted," I said quickly. Buck had told me that detail after. "Buck promised to continue Henry's legacy."

"There is no will," Maddox pointed out flatly. "We can't verify any of this. It's only that con man's word."

"He's not a con man," I said quietly, leaning on the counter. "He didn't steal money from that delicatessen in

New York. That was the owner's son. Buck saw him do it but didn't say anything because he didn't want to get the kid into trouble. Unfortunately, the kid had no such hesitation. When the theft came to light, he blamed Buck. Said he'd seen him take the money, and Buck was fired."

I'd gotten the whole story out of him earlier, and it had the ring of truth.

Maddox studied me for a long beat. "You've chosen to believe this guy and ignore the evidence. Buck Roberts had motive, means, and opportunity. I have to take him in."

"I know," I said, nodding. "But Buck didn't do it, and there's nothing concrete to say he did. His prints aren't on the knife. There were no witnesses to Henry's murder—other than Cocoa—and Buck's given a reasonable explanation for lying about when he arrived. If you check his messages, you'll see one from Henry a few weeks back."

Maddox's mouth flattened into a hard line, but I kept going, momentum carrying me forward.

"Thanks to Buck, we also know the peanut butter twists were made the night before. All the killer had to do was take them from the refrigerator and put them in the oven, knowing they'd start baking automatically at eight. Everything you've got on Buck is circumstantial."

Maddox narrowed his eyes. "You've been talking to your uncle, haven't you?"

I might have called him after speaking to Buck, just to get his advice.

"All I'm asking is that you keep an open mind," I said. "Buck is innocent, and he deserves to be treated that way until proven otherwise."

Maddox's jaw tightened. "I believe you've made your point, Miss Holloway."

Ah. We were back to *Miss Holloway*, were we?

I stood. "I'll go get Buck."

"Wait—you mean he's here?" Maddox shot to his feet so fast the barstool tipped backward. I caught it just in time and set it upright.

"Yes," I said calmly. "He's in my office."

Maddox just stared at me for a long moment, then shook his head slowly.

Chapter 35

Silvanthera montensis

"He took Buck into custody," Luke was telling Gina, who'd hurried over on her lunch hour after spotting the sheriff's Bronco parked outside my shop. We were huddled around the study table like conspirators, voices low. No one else was using the space—there was only one customer, a young woman leafing through a dark romance novel from the front display, oblivious to us.

"So they really think he did it?" Gina whispered, her tone hushed enough not to carry across the room.

"Yes, but they've got it wrong," I said firmly. Between the three of us, we filled her in on Buck's confession, every detail passed in subdued tones like we were trading state secrets.

"The poor man," she murmured, glancing from Luke to Carly, her brow creased. "I hope he's got a good lawyer."

"Well, until Henry's killer is caught, he's going to stay their prime suspect," I said sourly.

"And Monty's," Luke added, rubbing the back of his neck.

I nodded grimly. "That's the other thing that never sat right—Buck didn't even know Monty. Had no idea who he was."

"And we're pretty sure the two murders are related," Carly pointed out, leaning forward over the table.

Luke nodded in agreement, his expression taut.

"So if it wasn't Buck," Gina asked, "then who was it?"

"Someone who wanted Monty dead," I said, looking pointedly at Luke. "Henry was collateral. I think that's where we should be digging."

"But we've already ruled out Evie," Luke muttered, dropping his head into his hands. "I can't think of anyone else who'd want to hurt Monty."

"There's the thesis he hid in your room," I reminded him. "We still don't know why he did that. Could Evie shed any light?"

"What thesis?" Gina asked.

Luke told them about what he'd found.

"No, she didn't have any idea," he added.

"Do you have it with you?" Carly asked. "Can we see it?"

"I have it here." He rummaged through his backpack and pulled out a thick, printed manuscript in a clear plastic folder. The title page was missing, and according to Luke, this was only the second half of the paper. He set it down with a muted *thunk* on the study table. "I've been through it, but it's just botanical stuff. Plants. Woodland species. The names are all in Latin."

I picked it up and began flipping through slowly.

"Whose handwriting is this?" I asked, pointing to the messy scrawl that snaked through the margins of some typed pages.

"I don't know. Must be his tutor." Tess knew every senior year student was assigned one for their thesis.

"Wasn't Riley one of his professors?" Carly asked.

"Yes. Monty was his student," I said. "Riley's head of the botany department."

"Maybe he knows why Monty hid the manuscript?" Carly suggested.

I nodded. "Good point. I'll go see him this afternoon. I've managed to set an evening for his book signing, so I can use that as an excuse. Luke, want to come with me?"

"I can't. I've got classes."

"No problem," I said with a shrug. "He'll be happy enough to have a date for his signing."

"When's his book coming out?" Gina asked, more out of politeness than interest.

"Next week," I said. "The publisher pushed the release date forward. I'm not sure why."

"I guess it's a big deal if you're into plants," Carly shrugged. "Anyway, I've got to get back. Keep me posted and let me know if I can do anything for Buck. All that talent would be wasted inside."

She wasn't wrong.

The sky was an endless blue as I walked up to the science faculty building, my footsteps echoing off the pale stone steps. Inside, the air smelled faintly of coffee and copier toner. Students spilled through the corridor, chattering in clusters or gliding past with heads down and earbuds in. It must have been the change between classes. I sidestepped a group of freshmen laughing over something on a phone and made my way toward the botany department.

Riley's office door stood ajar, the brass nameplate gleaming: *Professor Adrian Riley – Department Head*. I knocked lightly and pushed it open.

Empty.

I lingered at the threshold. His desk was chaos—a sprawl of folders, battered reference books, and precarious towers of loose paper. A mug, stained with concentric rings of old coffee, sat too close to a pile of textbooks. I stepped inside.

I was here on legitimate business. I could wait in the chair like a normal person. That would be the *sensible* thing to do. But my gaze slid to the spread of papers across his desk.

Printouts, each one stamped "Final Proof" at the top, margins thick with a familiar, tightly packed handwriting— the same untidy scrawl I'd just seen in Monty's thesis. The professor's hand.

I inched a little closer until I could read the title: *Through the Canopy: The Discovery of* Silvanthera montensis.

I froze.

That name. *Silvanthera montensis.* It echoed through my mind. I'd seen it only hours ago in Monty's work, along with the same looping letters in the margin, the same pointed notes. My stomach tightened.

A glossy page peeked from beneath the proofs. I slid it free. It was a pre-publication review on letterhead from *The International Journal of Botany,* praising Riley's "groundbreaking identification and classification of a previously undocumented woodland species, *Silvanthera montensis.*" It hailed it as "a discovery that will reshape the field for decades."

My pulse quickened. Monty's thesis had been on this very plant. Had Riley lifted his student's research for his book? Was that why Monty had hidden it in Luke's room—because he was hiding it away from his own professor?

And if Riley *had* stolen it... had Monty confronted him? That would explain Monty's anxiety, his distraction of late.

A faint chill crawled over my skin. The room felt suddenly smaller. What I needed was evidence. I took out my phone and was about to take a photograph when a throat cleared behind me.

I swung around. Riley stood in the doorway, his eyes flicking from me to the paper in my hand. Slowly, he walked in, setting his leather satchel on a side table.

"What are you doing?" His tone was pleasant enough, but the undercurrent was steel.

"I was waiting for you," I said, forcing my voice to sound casual. I set the review page back on the desk. "I thought we could confirm the date for your signing."

His gaze lingered on the desk. "And while you waited, you decided to... what? Help me proofread?"

I ignored the barb. "I was actually wondering if you knew why Monty would hide part of his thesis. Luke found it in his room after he'd... died."

For a heartbeat, his face was still. Then the faintest muscle tick worked in his jaw.

"I think," he said slowly, "you already know the answer to that."

Someone walked past his office and said something. Riley turned to reply, his fake smile back in place.

I fumbled with my phone, just managed to hit the record button before he turned around again. The air between us seemed to thicken.

"Was it because of *Silvanthera montensis*?" I asked, my voice quieter now. "It's in Monty's work. Exactly the same plant species as in yours." I nodded to the proofs on his desk.

He smiled without humor. "Smart woman."

My heart was hammering. "You plagiarized him, didn't you? Monty made his discovery last year, but you've only just written this book."

Riley said nothing.

"Did he confront you?" I asked, a sick feeling in my stomach.

"That's none of your concern."

"It is if it got him killed."

Anger flickered in his expression, but it was quickly masked. "You've got it wrong, Miss Holloway. It was I who gave Monty the idea for his thesis, but he knew what I was working on and stole my idea. He was just a troubled kid who saw no other way out than to drown himself."

I slanted my gaze. "I suppose he hit himself on the head before he threw himself in the lake, did he?"

Rile shrugged. "How should I know?"

I stared at him and it suddenly all became clear. I saw the monster behind the spectacles. The charming academic façade was just that. An act. His eyes were as icy cold as the water that ran down into the lake from the glacier in winter.

"Did Monty threaten to report you? Plagiarism is a pretty serious offence. It would have ruined your career."

Riley stepped closer, slow and deliberate. He moved around the desk, closing the space between us until I could see the tiny flecks of gray in his blue eyes.

"Monty didn't know his place."

I shuddered. My instincts had been right.

"I knew there was the potential for a new species in these woods. I'd been looking for it for years."

"But he found it, didn't he? And you couldn't accept that. After all your searching, he was the one who was going to get the glory."

"And the academic grants, the funding for years of research. That was mine."

The hairs on my neck stood on end. Riley was unhinged. "So you killed him? You lay in wait and then hit him on the head so he was woozy, before pushing him into the lake. You tried to make it look like he drowned."

"Nearly got away with it too, until you started meddling." His voice was laced with venom.

I stared at him, knowing we were right all along. "But

Henry saw you, didn't he? You didn't expect him to be out walking his dog that early. He saw you murder Monty."

Riley shook his head. "That was regrettable. Henry was a friend. I liked him, but I knew he wouldn't keep his trap shut. He was a do-gooder, he'd go to the sheriff. I had to stop him."

I went cold. "So you followed him back to the bakery and stabbed him in cold blood."

Riley gave me a hard look. "You've got it all figured out, haven't you?"

"Not everything," I said. "How did you know about the automatic setting on the oven?"

He smirked. "That was a stroke of luck. Suzanne used to talk about Henry's routine, so I knew about the oven, even though I'd forgotten. It was only when I was there that I thought I'd put it to good use."

"So you took the peanut butter twist dough out of the refrigerator and put it in the oven, knowing it would switch on at eight o'clock."

"You got it, smarty pants."

"You were hoping we'd think Henry had still been alive when he put them in."

"That was the plan. I'd hoped it would lead that stupid sheriff astray. At eight o'clock I was here, in my office, you see. There are several students who will vouch for me."

It might have worked, if it had been the sheriff who'd been in charge of the case. "You must have known they'd do an autopsy and find out the real time of death?"

He shrugged. "It didn't really matter. Nobody could put me at the scene anyway. I was careful not to leave any evidence behind."

What would he say if he knew I'd recorded this whole conversation?

"So what now?" I whispered.

It was too late for him to do anything but finish me off. We both knew it. I knew the truth, so I had to die.

I still had my phone in my hand, behind my back. I had to call Luke, had to get help. This was going to go bad really fast, I could feel it.

Riley studied me for a long moment, as if weighing something, then he reached down and unlocked his desk drawer. Turning, I managed to fire off a quick SOS to Luke and slip the phone back into my pocket, before I heard the dull scrape of metal on wood. Then I saw it. The black snout of a pistol, and his hand wrapped around the grip.

My breath caught.

"Now," Riley said, voice low and calm, "you're going to come with me, and we're going to have a very different conversation."

Chapter 36

A Bad Smell

Cocoa

I smelled him before I saw him.

We were outside the science building, the air thick with the musty smell of books and damp leaves, when it drifted around the corner. Sharp, oily, and wrong. My nose twitched. My hackles prickled. I knew that smell.

That man.

He was the one who hurt Henry.

A low growl rumbled in my throat before I even thought about it. Then my paws moved on their own, faster than when I chase squirrels. Luke shouted my name, but I didn't stop. My legs pounded the pavement.

I rounded the corner just in time to see him. The bad man. His hand was on Tess's arm. She looked startled, her eyes wide. But before I could get to her, he shoved her into his car.

The door slammed. The engine roared. I barked, loud enough for the whole street to hear.

Luke's voice was behind me, urgent. He had the phone to his ear, talking fast to Detective Maddox. Maddox has a good smell—warm, steady, like pine and something faintly smoky. Luke asked if Maddox could track Tess. He must have a super-strong nose, since he wasn't even here.

Luke said to wait, but my paws were already moving. There was no time to wait. I wouldn't let Tess down. Not like I let Henry down. I hadn't gotten there in time for him, but I could still get there for her.

I chased the car. My ears streamed back in the wind, my breath loud in my head. The street blurred under me, the smell of exhaust filling my nose. A mile, maybe more, and then the car swerved onto a narrow road cutting into the woods.

My lungs burned. My legs ached. But as long as I could see that car, I could get to Tess.

But then—it was gone.

I skidded to a halt, sides heaving. I sniffed frantically, turning in circles, and then I caught it. A faint tang of oil and leather and something bitter. The man's smell. I pushed through undergrowth, following it, until there it was.

His car. Sitting quiet in the trees.

I ran up to it, pawing at the doors, but it was empty.

No man. No Tess.

I spun at the sound of wheels crunching gravel, but it was only Luke. He was on a bicycle, pedaling hard. He jumped off, his face flushed, and ran to me.

"Good work, boy!" he said, patting my head.

I wasn't a good boy. Not yet. I didn't have Tess back.

"Where is she?" he asked, crouching to look into my eyes. "Find Tess."

That was all I needed.

Her scent was here, I could smell it. Warm, familiar, with that faint trace of the soap she uses on her hands. I shot off into the trees, paws thudding on the packed earth. Luke followed on foot, crashing through the brush. The trail wound deeper, until a shape emerged through the branches. A cabin, weathered and quiet.

Luke was panting hard. He pulled out his phone again, muttering into it. "Maddox, I've found her. I'm sending you the location now." Struggling to catch his breath, Luke said, "Wait here, Cocoa. Maddox is on his way."

Wait?

What if something bad happened while we waited? What if it was like Henry?

I heard her voice. Tess's voice. A sharp, panicked cry. "No!"

My heart kicked.

That was it. I was going in.

I bolted, weaving around tree trunks, ducking under low branches. My paws tore through the last stretch of undergrowth. The cabin door was ajar. I lowered my head and shoved my shoulders against it. It swung inward.

The bad man was there, standing with his arm outstretched. At the end of it, a hard black thing. Tess sat on a chair in front of him, frozen. Her hands were behind her back, and her eyes were focused on the black thing in his hand. I could smell her fear.

I didn't think. I just leaped.

Straight for him.

Chapter 37

See You Around

I screamed as a charging ball of black fluff launched itself at Riley. It took a moment for me to realize it was Cocoa.

I'd never seen him like that before—he was a growling, frothing mass of pure aggression, his teeth clamped on Riley's arm as he shook it like a rag doll.

Riley let go of me, and the pistol clattered to the floor. My hands were still tied behind my back, secured to the chair, so I couldn't move. Riley was yelling, reaching for the gun with his free hand.

Oh no. Please don't let him shoot Cocoa.

I heard pounding footsteps outside, growing closer, and then in barreled the imposing figure of Detective Maddox, weapon drawn. One quick glance at the tangle of professor and dog on the floor, and he reacted like lightning. He kicked the gun out of Riley's reach and barked, "Let go, Cocoa. I've got him."

To my surprise, Cocoa obeyed, releasing Riley and turning to face Maddox. But the detective's attention was locked entirely on the man writhing on the floor, clutching his arm.

"Argh, my arm! That dog bit me. I need medical attention!" Riley howled.

"Get up!" Maddox growled, his gun steady. "Keep your hands where I can see them."

Cocoa trotted over to me and nudged me with his nose. Tears spilled down my cheeks—tears of sheer relief. I wasn't going to die after all.

"I'm okay, boy," I murmured, wishing I could hug him, but my hands were still bound. "Thank you. You saved me."

He sat down beside me, resolute, and didn't budge until Luke rushed in and untied me.

"Are you okay, Tess?" Luke asked.

I massaged my wrists. "Yeah, I'm fine."

My nerves were shot—I'd need a few strong mojitos to calm down—but I was alive, and that was all that mattered. I bent and buried my face in Cocoa's fur.

"Thank you for saving me," I whispered.

He wriggled, tail wagging so hard it thumped against Luke's leg, and then proceeded to lick my entire face. I laughed through my tears.

"Think you've got a friend for life there," Luke said.

He helped me to my feet, and we stepped outside. Maddox had cuffed Riley and was reading him his rights. Apparently, he'd already called for backup, and the sheriff was on his way.

"Thank you," I told Maddox once he'd handed Riley over to Grady and his deputy. They'd take him to the local jail and hold him until Maddox returned to question him.

"It was Luke and your furry friend here who did all the work," he said modestly. "I just came in at the end."

"Well, thank you anyway." I gave a shaky smile. "And before you say anything, I know it was foolish to go to his office, but I didn't realize it was him until I saw the papers on his desk."

Maddox frowned. "What papers?"

"The proofs for his new book. He was claiming to have discovered this new plant species, but it was actually Monty who found it. Riley was plagiarizing him. I got it all on tape."

"You did?" He stared at me.

"Yeah—it's on my phone, which you'll find near Riley's car. I didn't want him to get it, so I dropped it in the long grass."

Maddox chuckled. "Your uncle would be proud. Pity you didn't become a cop."

I grinned. "There's still time."

His eyes widened.

"Just kidding," I said before he could look truly alarmed. "I love being a bookseller. Nothing's going to change that."

"Glad to hear it."

He called Grady's deputy over and told him to find my phone. The kid hurried off, eager to impress the Boston detective.

I studied Maddox, an idea forming. "You know, Sheriff Grady is due to retire soon. Maple Ridge is going to need a new sheriff. Someone competent."

He narrowed his gaze. "What are you suggesting?"

I couldn't help but smile. "I think you know."

He didn't answer, but I could see the gears turning. It was a big leap—from the city to a small town like this—but his life in Boston hadn't been easy. Maybe he could use a change too.

"Just think about it," I urged. "We could use someone of your caliber here."

Grady strode over, cheeks flushed from the excitement. I doubted he'd ever arrested a murder suspect before. He'd be telling this story to his fishing buddies for years. I almost pitied them. "Ready to head out?" he asked Maddox.

The detective turned to me, and for a moment, his gaze softened. I caught a glimpse of the man he must have been before everything went wrong.

"See you around, Tess," he murmured.

I nodded. "See you around, Detective."

Then he turned to Grady and barked, "I'm ready. Let's go."

Chapter 38

Henry's Legacy

"So, it was Monty who discovered the new species of plant, not Professor Riley?" Carly asked the next day.

We were gathered at the bookstore's little coffee bar, mugs in hand, picking over the details one last time. The morning sunlight spilled through the front windows, catching the soft swirl of steam from our cups. Even Lindy had joined us, perching on a stool with her latte, clearly eager to hear my side of things.

"Yes," I said, glancing at Luke for confirmation. "Monty found it last year and built his thesis around it. Naturally, he told Riley, thinking his professor would be proud."

"Instead, Riley stole his discovery," Luke said, his jaw tight. "And when Monty threatened to report him, Riley killed him."

"Unfortunately, Henry had seen him at the lake," I added

quietly, my fingers curling around the warm mug in my hands. "So Riley came after him too."

"Poor Henry," Gina murmured, shaking her head. "If only he hadn't been walking Cocoa so early that morning."

"He was just in the wrong place at the wrong time," Luke muttered.

"What a terrible, terrible man," Carly said with a shudder. "And I thought he was quite charming—in a stodgy kind of way."

"You can never tell," I said. "Sometimes the most charming are the most rotten inside."

"You sound like you speak from experience," Lindy teased, arching a brow.

"I have an ex-husband," I quipped, earning a ripple of laughter. Only half a joke, really.

Gina had brought Iris along, and Cocoa and the pretty border collie were wrestling in the corner behind the till, tails wagging like metronomes.

"If you want them to stop, just say," Gina offered.

"No, they're fine." I smiled. The shop was quiet this early, no customers yet to mind the ruckus.

"Didn't Cocoa do well?" Lindy said fondly, watching the black Lab mock-charge Iris on his hind legs.

"He did. I still can't believe he found me," I admitted, my voice softening.

"Such a good boy," Lindy said as Iris zipped past him, looping back for more.

Gina turned back to me. "I can't believe you recorded the whole thing on your phone."

"I know. It was a spur-of-the-moment thing, but once I realized he was the killer, I knew I had to get evidence—just in case... well, just in case anything happened to me."

"It was very brave of you," Carly said. "I'd have just panicked and run away."

"I probably should have done that," I admitted with a grin.

Gina leaned forward. "Did you solve the mystery of the peanut butter twists?"

"Yes. Suzanne told Riley about the automatic oven. She likes to talk a lot in tutor sessions, so he knew all about Henry's routine. It only struck Riley when he was there to use it to his advantage. He thought if he ever needed an alibi, he could prove he was at work at eight o'clock."

"Very devious," Gina said.

"A bit short-sighted," Luke snorted. "I mean, with modern forensics, the police were definitely going to figure out the real time of death."

"Well, they can't always be so precise," Lindy pointed out. "There's usually a fairly wide window, particularly when the victim's been dead a while."

"Not this time," Luke replied.

She smiled at her student. "True."

"I guess your hunky detective had to let Buck go?" Carly asked, shooting me a sly grin.

"He is not 'my hunky detective,'" I said, but couldn't quite keep the corner of my mouth from twitching. "And yes, Buck's free. He came by last night to thank me."

"Buck is nice," Gina said. "I'm glad he's not a murderer."

"Me too. And he's promised to keep making peanut butter twists for the store."

"Ooh, where do I order?" Carly asked.

I grinned. "I'll give you his number."

Just then, Cocoa dashed across his bed, flipping it over in a burst of canine energy.

"Hey, Cocoa, settle down," I called, as Gina reached for Iris's lead.

"What's this?" Gina asked, straightening up with something in her hand. It was a tightly folded piece of paper.

I pursed my lips. "No idea. Where did you find it?"

"On the floor. I think it must have been stuck between the folds of Cocoa's bed."

I held out my hand. "Let me see."

She passed it over, and I unfolded it, curious to see what Cocoa had been sleeping on all this time. The paper was creased and faintly scented of dog. As soon as I smoothed it out, my breath caught.

"It's Henry's will."

"We found it!" Luke said, glancing across at me. "What does it say?"

A slow smile spread across my face. "He left the bakery—and everything in it—to Buck Roberts."

"Wow," Carly whispered.

"That's wonderful," Gina said softly. "He really did want Buck to continue his legacy."

I couldn't have been more pleased. "I know that's exactly what Buck will want to do."

I looked over at Cocoa, sitting beside his overturned bed, a sheepish expression on his face as if he knew exactly what he'd done. "Henry left it with the one he trusted most. You."

Cocoa whined and sidled over to me, resting his head heavily on my lap, his big eyes lifting to mine.

"Who's a good boy?" Gina gushed.

I bent down and wrapped my arms around him, burying my face in his fur. "He is. The best."

Outside, the street was waking up, Maple Ridge going about its day as if nothing terrible had happened here. But in that little moment, with Cocoa by my side and Henry's wishes safe in my hands, everything felt right again.

Ready for another mystery to solve? Click here to pre-order book two, *Paws and Prejudice*, or by using the link below!
https://a.co/d/0iOAIJ6e

Did you enjoy *The Peanut Butter Twist*? Leave a review to let us know your thoughts!
https://a.co/d/4VDcCwt

Tails of Maple Ridge Series

The Peanut Butter Twist

Paws and Prejudice

Also by Ellie Webster

* * *

Tails of Maple Ridge

The Peanut Butter Twist

Paws and Prejudice

Canine Confidential

The Barbershop Showdown

Old Tricks, New Trouble

Tangled Threads Mysteries

The Deadly Tapestry

Don't miss out on exclusive cozy content— sign up for the Ellie Webster newsletter today!

https://www.getdrip.com/forms/99805461/submissions/new

About the Author

Ellie Webster is the shared pen name for a small group of writers who adore all things cozy and mysterious. Set in the picturesque towns of New England, Ellie's stories feature lovable amateur sleuths, loyal pets, and plenty of twists tucked between cups of coffee and community gossip. Expect warmth, wit, and a mystery that keeps you turning the pages long after lights-out.

Perfect for readers who enjoy a steaming mug beside them, a faithful cat or dog at their feet, and the comforting promise that justice (and a slice of pie) will always be served.

instagram.com/authorelliewebster

tiktok.com/@authorelliewebster